I0571118

THE BEEBLES REFRAIN,
Another Testament of Time and Art

by Lowery Christopher Collins

THIS VOLUME CONTAINS BOTH
THE FULL-LENGTH VERSION
OF THE SCRIPT
<u>AND</u> THE CUT,
40-MINUTE VERSION
OF THE SCRIPT.

THE BEEBLES REFRAIN,
ANOTHER TESTAMENT OF TIME AND ART

BY LOWERY CHRISTOPHER COLLINS

Ponderlake Publishing

THE BEEBLES REFRAIN,
ANOTHER TESTAMENT OF TIME AND ART

Written by Lowery Christopher Collins

Copyright © 2020 by Lowery Christopher Collins

Ponderlake Publishing: www.ponderlake.com

Playwright and/or Royalty Information: www.ChristopherCollinsOnline.com

ISBN 978-0-9992241-2-0

Ponderlake
Publishing

FULL-LENGTH and ONE-ACT VERSIONS

This volume contains both the full-length copy of the play and the under-40-minute copy (the entire script, but with permissible strikethroughs.)

The full-length play begins on page 15.

The under-40-minute version begins on page 60.

USING THE UNDER-40 VERSION

If a group or organization wishes to performed a one-act version of the play, the second version with the approved strikethroughs must be used.

The Beebles Refrain,

Another Testament of Time and Art

by Lowery Christopher Collins

9M, 2F

CAST of CHARACTERS (in order of appearance):

Man

SM

Montaño

Piddles

Michael

Hatch

Agatha

Match

Law

FO

Grim

PLEASE READ THESE NOTES BEFORE EVEN READING THE PLAY—

Note About This SEQUEL: This play, "The Beebles Refrain, Another Testament of Time and Art," is the SEQUEL to "The Beebles Accord, a Dramatic Treatise of Time and Art." Although readers, producers, directors, actors, and even potential audiences are encouraged to have read or seen "The ACCORD" before watching or attempting "The REFRAIN," such a pre-knowledge is not necessary. This play is written in such a way that audiences can share "The REFRAIN" experience independently of its predecessor. In fact, the characters in *this* show specifically explain to each other (and thereby to the audience) any information absolutely *necessary* to know from the first show.

Note About the PRODUCTION of the SHOW: Note to potential directors: as is the case of "The Beebles Accord," when producing "The Beebles Refrain," please remember that while the shows being parodied should be done so with as much *fun and exaggeration* as possible, they must also be shown the proper respect. The show references are not mentioned to mock the plays, but rather to pay homage to them and to address them in a lighthearted manner. Also, while this play is, at times, farcical, please don't forget that it does contain a message beyond the humor, that all of us in the theatre world have a responsibility and an honor to create art on stage.

A few of the works respectfully parodied in "The Beebles Refrain" are:

"The Beebles Accord"	"The Tragedy of Doctor Faustus"
"Macbeth"	"Medea"
	"Dancing at Lughnasa"
"Our Town"	"The Miracle Worker"
Sondheim's "Company"	"Oedipus Rex"
"Moon Over Buffalo"	"The Curious Incident of the Dog in the Night-
"Julius Caesar"	Time"
"Les Misérables"	"Equus"
"Noises Off"	"Arsenic and Old Lace"
"The Importance of Being Earnest"	"Cyrano de Bergerac"
"Rosencrantz and Guildenstern Are Dead"	"Death of a Salesman"
"The Merchant of Venice"	"Romeo and Juliet"
"Richard III"	"Hamlet"

as well as gentle references to

"The Little Mermaid," "Harry Potter," *Moby Dick*, the artist Prince, Heath Ledger, Brecht, Tennessee Williams, George Bernard Shaw, *Moulin Rouge*, Billy Joel, Queen, and many more

Full-Length Version

The Beebles Refrain,
Another Testament of Time and Art

The set should be multilevel, providing a place that will eventually be a path on a mountaintop. It's recommended that various set pieces pertaining to theatre be placed on stage: theatre signs, etc. Also, it's best if ladders with clocks are placed on the stage, echoing the mood of the "Accord." If possible, the words "Time" and "Art" should be visible to the audience. A bench is needed as well, preferably downstage left.

In order to have ideal effect, this show needs various play-related images projected on a cyclorama during the show.

In the darkness, ominous music starts playing. A blue light gradually rises. Fog fills the air. There is a loud knocking. Five knocks. There is a pause. Five more knocks. The sound of a man's voice BEGINNING off stage.

Man.   (*Entering, speaking with a Scottish brogue*) Knock, knock, knock! Who's there, i' the name of Beelzebub? Here's a farmer that hanged himself on the expectation of plenty.

The knocking continues.

Man.   Knock, knock! Who's there, in the other devil's name?

Knocking within

Man.   Knock, knock, knock! Who's there? Faith, here's an English tailor come hither, for stealing out of a French hose: come in, tailor; here you may roast your goose.

Knocking within

Man.   Knock, knock; never at quiet! What are you? But this place is too cold for hell.

The man opens the gate. Another man, THE STAGE MANAGER, walks in. He is backlit.

SM.   This play is called "The Beebles Refrain, Another Testament of Time and Art.'

Man.   Who are you?

SM.   You know who it's written, produced, and directed by. You should have programs. (*Looks around*) The name of this place is Dunsinane, Scotland, as you may have figured out, just north of Hadrian's Wall, the latitude and the longitude uncertain, since, of course, it's fictitious.

Man.   Fictitious?

SM.   This one-act is a parody. Just like the original "Beebles ACCORD," it contains all kinds of theatre and play references that most people don't catch—as we've learned, even people who should catch them sometimes don't. This particular play is called "M . . ."

Man.   No! Are ye mad an' off yer bonkers, ye crazy man, ye?

SM.   What?

Man.   Ye c'nno' say the name of the play. You're supposed to call it "The Sco'ish Play."

SM.   First, there are many Scottish plays. Second, I don't believe in silly superstitions. And last, we're currently in the actual play. Even if people adhere to crazy ways, you're allowed to use the name during the performance.

Man.   Is that a fact?

SM.   I'm the Stage Manager. I know these things.

Man.   The Stage Ma'ager?

SM.   The Stage Manager. Created by Thornton Wilder. 1901. Grover's Corners. The Stage Manager.

Man.   Oh.

SM.   Yes.

Man.   Well, I defer to you.

SM.   Where was I?

Man.   Discussing Dunsinane.

SM.   I don't think that's right.

Man.   Aye. It *was* right; you were talking about this great castle.

SM.   Are you sure? I was certain I was talking about something verboten and taboo. I just can't remember. You've disturbed my internal vibrations.

Man.   Your what? And speak English, would you! Don't use none of those fancy stage-manager words on me.

16

SM.   May I please continue?

Man.   Nobody's stoppin' ye.

SM.   Ah, yes. I remember. The *play* references throughout this script! This particular script is one that most audiences are aware of, from the witches' brew to Burnham Wood, from the ghost of Banquo to the unwashable spot, we start with one of Shakespeare's master works, "The Tragedy of . . ."

Man.   You're going to tempt fate again?

SM.   "Macbeth."

The Man looks around, as if anticipating death or for one of its lesser brothers to appear.

The SM looks around defiantly.

SM.   What are you doing? There's nothing happening. I'm standing here.

The Man pokes the SM's arm from a distance.

SM.   See. I'm still here. There is no curse.

Out of nowhere, a baseball comes and hits the SM, causing him to fall out as if dead.

Man.   (*wide-eyed*) Ooooooooooooooooooooooh. I told ye so! You be dancin' on ye mum's grave with that kind of rebellion. (*looks around, then bends down to whisper loudly to SM*) Don't say I did't warn ye! (*Beat*) Do you be being alive? Listen there, lad! Are you being alive? Did someone hold you too close? Did someone hurt you too deep? Ye catch that reference, Neil Patrick?

Montaño.   (*Entering*) Anybody seen my ball? Wait, is this . . . ? The show hasn't begun yet, has it?

Man.   Ay, there was already the knocking at the gate, and this poor unfortunate soul wantin' to be where the people are and callin' himself the Stage Manager came in and started talking all his gobbledy gook.

Montaño looks at the SM.

Montaño.   The Stage Manager? What? What's wrong with him? He looks . . .

Man.   He was talkin' and talkin' and actually said the *real* name of the Sco'ish play, the name that shall not be named, the cursed title of the Voldemort of Shakespeare. Then this white thing came out of nowhere and hit him. Down he went.

Montaño.   My ball hit him?

Man.   Was that wha' it was? Oh. Sounds like a personal problem to me.

Montaño.   Oh, man. It's not . . . No, it's not . . . And the play *started* already? It wasn't supposed to . . .

17

Man.   I've told ye before. The show began. The Stage Manager here called it
                (*searching*) "The Beebles . . . Refrain" or somet'in' like that.

Montaño slowly looks out over the audience, realizing that there IS an audience.

Montaño.   Oh, man. Jiminy Cricket on a pogo stick! They're here and watching. (*yelling*)
                Guys! GUYS! Get out here quick! GUYS!!

*Michael, Piddles, and Hatch come onto the stage, finishing putting on their costumes, putting a
layer of giant furry cloaks on top of their nice, theatre attire.*

Piddles.   What's wrong, Montaño? We're trying to get these monstrosities on to cover up
                our nice clothes, like we did with the Chalk Circle. These Scottish Play pieces are
                too heavy, though. I don't know if we even need them.

Michael.   What's going on? (*referring to the Stage Manager*) Who's he?

Montaño.   The Stage Manager. *The* Stage Manager.

Michael.   The Stage Manager? (*Beat*) From "Our . . ."

Montaño.   From our play.

Michael.   What's he doing like that?

Montaño.   (*subtly pointing to the audience*) Look out there.

Michael.   What?

Montaño.   Look. Out. There.

Piddles.   What are *they* doing out there?

Montaño.   The play already started several minutes ago.

Michael.   What?

Hatch.   It what?

Man.   He started knocking. I had to go and open it. These people were waiting. The
                eerie music and stage lighting had already begun as well. That person in black
                back there pointed at me and said it was my cue.

Michael.   (*Referring to The Stage Manager*) What's wrong with him?

Piddles.   Michael, we have to join the show in progress.

Michael.   What *happened* to him?

Piddles.   (*looking out over the audience*) Michael, we have to start acting. It's
                already started.

Montaño.   I think I accidently hit him with my baseball.

18

Michael.   What?

Piddles.   Oh, Montaño! Have you already killed someone?

Hatch.   The horror.

Montaño.   Does that mean . . . ?

Piddles.   I'm afraid so.

Hatch.   So, we're expecting . . . ?

Michael.   And so early in the script.

Agatha enters.

Agatha.   Do I sense a sense of resistance to my insistence to make an entrance?

Piddles.   What?

Man.   Is this woman a poet?

Agatha.   Many have wondered. And many have rightfully been in awe. But I'm just a world-class writer, a novelist, a playwright, a solver of mysteries, a master of the enigmas presented by murder.

Michael.   We know, Agatha. We know who you are. It's us. And . . . you.

Piddles.   We haven't seen you since Beebles showed up at the end of the last play.

Agatha.   I know. We haven't been on stage since then.

Piddles.   True. Come to think of it, that's the last time we were all together.

Michael.   It's the last time we could be together. That's when our characters last saw each other. *But* I'm more concerned about the Stage Manager.

Agatha.   Ooooh! Get ready for it. This man looks dead.

Michael.   But he can't be.

Montaño.   No, he can't be. Please don't be.

Piddles.   Nobody blames you, Montaño. It was an accident.

Michael.   You don't understand what I'm saying. He *can't* be dead. Haven't you read "Our Town"? He's immortal. The Stage Manager . . .

Agatha.   Looks pretty dead to me.

Hatch.   This isn't good.

Agatha.   Oh, Hatch. Hello. Where's your twin?

Hatch.   (*Lip quivering from being upset*) Match?

19

Agatha.   Yes, Hatch. Where's Match?

Hatch.   (*starts crying*) He left.

Agatha.   I'm sorry. I didn't mean to . . .

Piddles.   (*comforting Hatch*) It's just a touchy subject. Match just . . .

Hatch.   He went to find himself. He didn't want to be known as one half of
             "the twins." He wasn't content to be *Match*. He went to . . . (*sobbing*)

Agatha.   Where?

Piddles.   Buffalo.

Agatha.   New York?

Montaño.   No, Texas. He wanted to remake himself. Get a tan. There's a good *sun* over
             Buffalo.

Michael.   Can we focus on this man?

Man.   Me? Want to focus on me?

Michael.   What? No. The Stage Manager.

Man.   Because I'm the man, you know. That's my actual name.   Even in the script.
             Probably in the "Beebles Refrain" text itself. I'm the generic man who does
             what's needed for the scene, to help it along.

Hatch.   Wait. That's what my brother and I were.   We were the lackies, the aesthetic
             element, the sidekicks.

Man.   Well, evidently, you're no longer a team.

Hatch.   (*crying*) Match.

Piddles.   (*to Man*) Stop!

Man.   Can I become your brother?

Hatch.   What? No!

Man.   I'd really like a name.

Michael.   Can we please focus on the problem at hand? The clock is ticking.

Agatha.   (*Proclaiming*) This man is . . .

SM.   (*Getting up*) Very much alive.

Everyone jumps back a bit.

20

Agatha.   Drat.

Piddles.   Here we go again.

Michael.   What's going on?

SM.   I was just lying there, listening to everything you've been saying.

Montaño.   You're alive! (*He hugs the SM*)

SM.   (*Uncomfortable with the hug*) I'm the Stage Manager. I can't die. Now please get off of me.

Montaño releases him.

Michael.   That's what I said.

Piddles.   That's what he said. (*realizing that the "That's what she said" joke doesn't work with the he pronoun*) Oh, it doesn't work that way, does it?

Hatch.   No.

Michael.   (*to SM*) Why? Why would you do that?

SM.   Well, I was indeed hit by a baseball, evidently from Montaño here.

Montaño.   Sorry.

SM.   It knocked the wind out of me. But when you all came up, I wanted to see what your intentions were, why you weren't already out on stage when the show started.

Michael.   You started it early.

SM.   I'm the Stage Manager.

Piddles.   We didn't have time to get all the cloaks on. You could have waited.

SM.   I'm the Stage Manager.

Man.   Are we going on with the Sco'ish play?

SM.   Yes.

Michael.   I'm the leader of this troupe now. This play, this script, this series of scripts— they're our home.

SM.   But I'm . . .

Michael.   Not the real stage manager. You're the character "The Stage Manager."

SM.   Don't confuse me. (*looking to the audience*) Or them.

Michael.   (*Takes a deep breath*) Places everyone. (*To the Stage Manager*) You, too.

21

Everyone builds a tableau, looking toward the Stage Manager, as he begins.

SM.   This play, this play within the parody, this referenced work . . .

Hatch.   We get it.

SM.   Is set in rural Scotland during dark ages of humanity's past.

We hear various farm animals bleating, neighing, etc.

SM.   A time in which . . .

Piddles.   Did I just hear Beebles?

Michael.   You couldn't have.

Hatch.   I thought I heard her, too.

Michael.   Beebles isn't here.

Agatha.   It sure sounded like her bellow to me, too.

Montaño.   (*to the audience*) For those of you who may not know or who may not remember, Beebles is a very special cow that was missing in "The Beebles Accord." At the end of the play, she returned to her owner, our friend, Colton, even though a few original audience members didn't listen to all the cow references.

Michael.   Montaño.

Montaño.   A young man even said out loud after the standing ovation, "Oh! Beebles is a cow!"

Michael.   Montaño.

Montaño.   So, yeah, Beebles is a cow. Jus' sayin'. (*self-satisfied*) I'm finished.

SM.   May I please continue?

Michael.   Look, I'd like it to be her just as much as you. When I met her, I understood. She brings a certain peace. But she's not here.

Piddles.   This play *is* called "The Beebles *Refrain.*" Doesn't that mean that there's a repetition?

Hatch.   Yeah.

Agatha.   That is the definition.

Michael.   (*to Hatch and Agatha*) You're getting her hopes up.

Agatha.   What are you talking about?

Michael.   (*pulling Agatha aside*) Colton. You do remember Colton? The one Piddles loved? The boy looking for his cow?

22

Agatha.   Yes, that *was* part of the premise of the first play.

Michael.   He found Beebles.

Agatha.   I know. I was there.

Michael.   And then he ran off and married a super model named Amber.

Agatha.   What?

Michael.   He married a super model. He's living in Paris now.

Agatha.   Wait. I thought he . . .

Michael.   Wasn't interested in Piddles?

Agatha.   I thought he wasn't interested . . .

Michael.   . . . in Piddles.

Agatha.   Oh.

Hatch.   (*Walking up*) He did have a good sense of style, though.

Piddles.   Are you talking about me?

Michael.   (*taking leadership*) This play covers all new references.

Man.   Can I change roles now?

SM.   Not yet.

Michael.   New play.

SM.   But . . .

Michael.   New play.

Piddles.   You're taking this new leadership role seriously.

Michael.   That's my job. We bring words to life. We bring art to life. All that jazz. Right?

Piddles.   Sexy.

Michael.   And our job, yet again, is to present it all, the good and the bad, the uplifting, and the dark.

Michael hands a tunic to SM.

The others scramble for tunics.

Michael.   (*to SM, giving him his line*) The Ides of March are come.

SM.   Now?

Michael.   (*to SM, insistent*) The Ides of March are come.

23

SM.   (*sighing*) The Ides of March are come.

Michael.   (*as Soothsayer*) Ay, Caesar, but not gone.

The characters create a tableau of Roman Senators preparing for the entrance of Caesar.

Piddles.   (*as Cassius*) What, urge you your petitions in the street? Come to the capitol.

SM.   Do I have to?

Michael.   Yes!

SM walks around the stage and ends up where he was when he started. The other actors follow him.

Piddles.   I could be well moved if I were you, but I am constant as the northern star.

Man.   O Caesar.

SM.   Oh, me.

Hatch.   Great Caesar!

SM.   Doth not Brutus bootless kneel?

Agatha.   Speak, hands for me!

SM.   Here it comes.

Montaño.   From the pits of hell, I stab at thee!

Michael.   That's *Moby Dick*.

Montaño.   I know. Whale of a book. (*He laughs. No one joins his laughter.*)

Agatha, the Man, Hatch, Montaño, and Piddles stab SM.   Then Michael stabs him.

SM.   Et tu, Brute! Then fall, Caesar!

SM, as Caesar, falls dead.

Man.   Liberty! Freedom! Tyranny is dead!

Piddles.   (*singing*) Do you hear the people sing? Singing the songs of angry men?

Michael.   It's not time for a song. And we overkilled *Les Mis* last time.

Piddles.   Sorry.

Man.   Liberty! Freedom! Tyranny is dead!

Michael.   You already said that.

Man.   Oh, okay.

Montaño.   Your Scottish dialect is gone.

Man.   I was acting.

Agatha.   He's an actor.

Montaño.   I know that.

Michael.   Caesar is dead! I told you he was ambitious!

Montaño.   You did. Quite well. We didn't hear it in this script, but you did say it. I read it in high school English.

Match enters and begins a monologue.

Match.   Friends, Romans, countrymen!

Hatch.   Match!! (*Running up to him*)

Match holds up his palm to stop him. Hatch stops.

Match.   (*reverent, sincere*) Friends, Romans, countrymen, lend me your beers.

Michael.   Ears.

Match.   Your ears.

Montaño.   (*laughing*) He said "beers."

Match.   (*Continuing*) I come to bury Caesar, not to praise him. The evil that men do lives after them. The good is oft interred with their bones; So let it be with Caesar.

Hatch claps. Match holds out his hand to stop him.

Match.   The noble Brutus hath told you that Caesar was ambitious.

Michael.   I did.

Piddles.   He did.

Match.   I'll tell you what's ambitious.

Montaño.   Uh-oh. He's going off script.

Match.   Ambition is taking on the responsibility of doing what we're doing on this stage.

Piddles.   What?

Match.   I've had a lot of time to think. And I thought and I've read and I've looked and I've thought. And in looking for myself, I found truth.

Hatch.   You have? I'm proud of you, brother.

Agatha.   You *have* become more talkative.

Match.   I've thought a lot about Beebles.

25

Michael. Match . . .

Match. Wait. I know we were looking and looking, and she came to us. She showed up so we could see her, but I don't know if doing all the shows and searching for why we're doing it and . . . (*gets overwhelmed*)

Michael. You're experiencing a crisis like I did. I understand, Match. It's normal.

Match. Why do we do this? We memorize and get on this stage, in this moment.

Piddles, Montaño, and Hatch all stomp a rhythmic stomp.

Piddles. Sorry. Old habits.

Match. I worry people won't understand the shows.

SM. The references.

Match. Who are you?

SM. The Stage Manager.

Match. No, you're not. I just talked with the stage manager.

Michael. The character of the Stage Manager.

Match. See? (*frustrated*) Confusion.

Michael. Not everybody's going to understand everything. That's okay. We keep going, show after show. We do this glorious task. Remember?

Match. Who are you trying to convince?

Michael. (*Taken back a bit*) Remember?

Match. I want to remember. I want to get it.

Montaño. Maybe we should just *do* it?

Piddles. What do you mean?

Montaño. Quit talking. Quit elaborating. Just run these babies. These are all new *references*, right?

Michael. Right. That's why we're here. I've learned that lesson. We create, but learn from the shows.

SM. References.

Montaño. Whatever. Just go. Let's do it. Go!

Piddles. He's right.

Michael. (*to Match*) Are you able to do this?

Match.   Maybe.

Michael.   What about handling bigger roles?

Match.   I'll try.

Montaño.   Excellent. Go!

Agatha.   Wait. Where are Mary Ann and Brannon?

Piddles.   (*Obviously trying to avoid the question*) It doesn't matter.

Agatha.   What? What do you mean? Where are they?

Piddles.   People move on. Characters move on. We're written for this moment on this
             stage.

Man.   Who are Mary Ann and Brannon?

Agatha.   Characters in "The Beebles Accord"

Piddles.   (*Sorrowfully*) Mary Ann's character is written out. The actress has moved on.
             (*Beat*) And . . . Brannon . . . (*pauses*) is dead.

Hatch.   What?

Agatha.   Dead?

Piddles.   (*Quickly*) The playwright wrote another short play between these two. (*Almost in
             tears*) He put Brannon in it and killed him off.

Match.   What?

Hatch.   How awful!

Agatha.   How delicious.

Piddles.   It was noble. His end was . . . heroic, but Brannon is no more. He was a
             character.

Hatch.   Aren't we all . . . (*realizing his own "character mortality"*) oh.

Montaño.   Can we move on? Time's wasting. We're going hyper-speed. With your
             permission, Michael?

Michael.   Go.

Piddles.   Hyper-speed?

Michael.   Let's try it.

*One of the characters runs offstage to retrieve a telephone that is given to Michael (for him to
hold for the upcoming scene) and a plate of sardines that is given to Agatha. Also, someone
needs to get a chair or stool for SM to "direct" from DR.*

27

Agatha. *(Runs downstage, speaks in a deep British brogue)* And I take the sardine. No, I leave the sardines. No, I take the sardines.

SM. *(Joining her, looking out over the audience to answer her)* You leave the sardines and you hang up the phone.

Michael. Wait. We can't do this play.

Agatha. Yes, right. I hang up the phone.

Michael. Agatha.

SM. And you leave the sardines.

Agatha. I leave the sardines?

Michael. Agatha! *(searching for the Stage Manager's name here)* SM!

SM. SM?

Michael. I don't know what else to call you. Your character is . . . ?

SM. *(Certain of the answer, then hesitating, confused.)* Uh. Yeah. Uh.

Michael. SM.

SM. Okay.

Agatha. But I like this play. I want to play Dotty. It's the first role I've felt this connected to since we began.

Michael. Look around. We don't have the set.

Agatha. We don't need . . . oh.

SM. Yeah, the set *is* a major part.

Montaño. Can we move on?

During this part, characters need to take the plate of sardines and move the director's chair off-stage.

Michael. We'll find some way to make "Noises Off" work, just not now. We'll have to build a set.

Agatha. Is that a promise?

Michael. It is. Just not now.

Match. Everything is falling apart. I knew it.

Piddles. C'mon everybody. Come with me. Let's let Michael and Match tackle this next part.

Match.   No, don't leave. I don't know if I'm up for it. I need you guys here.

Piddles.   Okay. We'll sit then.

Everyone besides Michael and Match sits on the set.

Michael.   Okay, Match. Think about it. We're staying in Europe. It's the 1890's. High society. The end of the Victorian Age.

Man.   I know what *this* is.

Piddles.   Shh.

Michael.   Everything is about appearances and status.

Montaño.   It's wild. Get it? (*Giggles*)

Piddles.   Shh, Montaño.

Match.   Michael, I'm not into it.

Michael.   Yeah, you are. You can do it. (*acting, British accent*) Besides, your name isn't Jack at all; it's Ernest.

Match.   Oh.

Michael.   C'mon. You know the line.

Match.   I don't remember it.

Michael.   "It isn't Ernest; it's Jack."

Match.   Oh, okay. Sorry.

Michael.   No, that's your line.

Match.   What is?

Michael.   "It isn't Earnest; it's Jack."

Match.   Oh, okay. (*British accent*) It isn't Ernest; it's Jack.

Michael.   (*Acting*) You have always told me it was Ernest. I have introduced you to everyone as Ernest. You answer to the name of Ernest. You look as if your name was Ernest. You are the most earnest-looking person I ever saw in my life. It is perfectly absurd that your name isn't Ernest. It's on your cards. Here is one of them. (*He pulls out a card and starts to read.*) Mr. . . .

Match.   (*grabs the card out of his hand*) No.

Michael.   You're not supposed to do that. I have to read the card. I don't have that part memorized.

Match.   No. I can't do this.

Piddles.   (*walking up*) Match, what's wrong? Are you okay?

SM.   He said he wasn't into it.

Montaño.   That can't stop us.

Michael.   No, it can't. Not being in the mood to act can never keep an actor from acting. Never. We have a duty. We are in the shows that we . . . are in.

SM.   And you're not into it, either.

Michael.   What?

SM.   I can tell. Your heart isn't in it.

Michael.   Look. You're new here. You don't know me. I admit that I wasn't always where I should be, but I've matured. I know what it means to be a mature actor now.

SM.   Do you?

Montaño.   Watch your attitude, bud!

SM.   Or what? You're going to hit me with another baseball?

Montaño.   Is that a request? I can comply!

Piddles.   Calm down, now. Calm down.

Michael.   (*Frustrated*) I'm faithful. I'm here on this stage, doing what I know we have to do.

Piddles.   We know, Michael. We know.

SM.   Do we?

Montaño.   (*to Piddles, looking at SM)* Let me take him out.

Piddles.   No.

Hatch.   No more violence!

Montaño.   There hasn't been any violence. Yet.

SM.   Baseball.

Man.   That *was* pretty cool.

Michael.   Enough! We're not here to play around. We have a task. As Brannon told us last time, the playwright's given us the responsibility to cover the shows, the references. And Match, you can do it, too.

Match.   But some of these, even *I* don't understand.

Michael.	We'll work through it. It's all a mystery, right? There are things that don't make sense.
Agatha.	Like a flipped coin?
Michael.	What?
Piddles.	Always on heads?
Michael.	Always on . . . oh! Yeah. (*pretends to flip a coin over and over*) Heads. Heads. Come on!
Montaño.	The law of averages, if I have this right, means that if six monkeys were thrown up in the air for long enough they would land on their tails about as often as they would land on their . . .
Man.	Heads!
SM.	(*Stepping up on the set*) I will buy with you, sell with you, talk with you, walk with you, and so following, but I will not eat with you, drink with you, nor pray with you. For, if you prick us, do we not bleed? If you tickle us, do we not laugh? If you poison us, do we not die? And if you wrong us, shall we not revenge?
Piddles.	Very nice. Very nice.
Michael.	Not bad.
Montaño.	I'd like to see him try Shylock, though.
Hatch.	That was Shylock.
Montaño.	I mean Shylock from "The Merchant of Venice."
Hatch.	That *was* Shylock.
Agatha.	From "The Merchant of Venice."
Montaño.	Well, it didn't sound like it. I would have chosen the part about a horse, of course, of course.
Piddles.	What?
Montaño.	In "The Merchant of Venice" when Shylock is in desperation. He says, "Every tale condemns me for a villain." A horse of course, of course, my kingdom, of course.
Michael.	Montaño, that's "Richard III."
Montaño.	I don't care if he said it three or even four times.
Michael.	No, the play, "Richard III." And it's "a horse, a horse, my kingdom for a horse."

Montaño.   I get something a little mixed up, and everybody goes nuts.

Michael.   It's okay. We're just getting it all straight.

Match.   (*affecting a hunched back*) Now is the winter of our discontent, made glorious summer by this sun of York.

Hatch.   Match, that's great.

Match.   I actually know that one. I played Richard years ago.

Piddles.   Really?

Match.   Believe it or not, I did.

Man.   (*to Michael*) Can he *do* that?

Michael.   What?

Man.   Play Richard with the *back problem*, you know.

Michael.   As a hunchback?

Man.   Shhh! Can you say that?

Michael.   For *now*. That's Richard III. It's a part of Shakespeare's character. It's an integral part of the script.

Hatch.   (*to Match*) You'd better drop the back thing now. It could be offensive.

Match.   It's fun.

Hatch.   Not if it were real.

Match straightens up.

Montaño.   You all know what's next!

Agatha.   I forgot.

SM.   Me, too. What's he talking about.

Montaño.   All *hell's* gonna break loose!

Piddles.   Language! You can't say that.

Montaño.   If it's literal, yes, I can. You know what's coming!

Agatha.   Oh!

Montaño.   Get ready to bust up through the floor. We're going back to the 1500's again!

Michael.   Okay, Montaño. Get ready.

Montaño.   Oh, I'm ready.

Michael. (*while everyone is scrambling to get low on the floor at various places*) Match, remember that you're coming to collect him.

Match. Wait. What? Me? Oh, those are my lines?

Montaño. Match, you know these!

Match. No, wait. I don't. I knew Richard, but I don't know these.

Michael. You've got it. They'll come to you. Go, Montaño.

Montaño. Was this the face that launch'd a thousand ships? And burnt the topless towers of Ilium? Sweet Helen, make me immortal with a kiss. (*laughs*)

Michael. (*to Match*) That's your line.

Match. I don't know it.

Michael. Yes, you do.

Match. No, I don't.

Montaño. (*repeating himself*) Sweet Helen, make me immortal with a kiss. (*laughs*)

Michael. Match!

Law enters with stealth and power and takes over Match's part.

Law. Thus to we ascend to view those souls which sin seals the black souls of hell. And, this gloomy night, here in his room, will wretched Faustus be.

Montaño. What shall become of Faustus, being in hell forever? God forbade it, indeed; but Faustus hath done it: for the vain pleasure of four-and-twenty years hath Faustus lost eternal joy and felicity. I writ them a bill with mine own blood: the date is expired; this is the time, and he will fetch me.

Law. What, weep'st thou? 'tis too late; despair! Farewell: Fools that will laugh on earth must weep in hell.

Montaño. Impose some end to my incessant pain; Let Faustus live in hell a thousand years, A hundred thousand, and at last be sav'd! No end is limited to damned souls.

The other actors as devils come and start to pull Montaño down below the set—or upstage.

Montaño. I'll burn my book! Ahhh!!

The all come up for air. They congratulate Montaño and hug Law.

Piddles. Law!

Michael. Law, how are you?

Hatch. I didn't expect to see you.

33

Agatha.   How did I know you couldn't stay away?

Law.   Well, you needed a devil, and what better character than a lawyer?

Match.   Good point.

Man.   Who is this?

Piddles.   This is Law, our friend from the first . . . show about Beebles.

Law.   Where is Beebles?

Hatch.   She's with Colton.

Law.   I heard about the Swedish supermodel.

Piddles.   What?

Agatha.   She was Swedish?

Michael.   Let's change the subject.

Piddles.   A few of us heard Beebles earlier.

Michael.   It wasn't Beebles.

SM.   It was definitely a cow's bellow.

Michael.   It wasn't. It could have been anything.

Hatch.   It was a bellow.

Michael.   Law, it's best to drop it.

Law.   You know, a lot has happened since the last Beebles' show.

Michael.   Well, technically, when the lights went out, the show ended, and nothing in this reality has happened again until this one, the "Beebles Refrain" began.

Law.   So, that's what he called it? "The Beebles Refrain." Clever. Good. But there were events between the two shows. I see that you've become a leader, Michael.

Michael.   I'm trying.

Hatch.   We lost a few people.

Law.   I heard.

Piddles.   You know about it?

Law.   I was in the show with Brannon. It was a short ten-minute play, but I was there.

Piddles.   I didn't know.

Law.   It's okay. It was a special time, and because of it, I've been searching for myself.

SM.   Just what we need: another one of you going all emotionally unstable.

Law.   Who's this?

Montaño.   Nobody.

SM.   I'm The Stage Manager.

Michael.   From the first show we referenced.

Law.   Ah. "Our Town"?

Michael.   Yeah.

Law.   Okay. (*ignoring SM*) For the record, I'm not emotionally unstable. I'm just coming to grips with the nature of being a character. Michael, I understand what you were dealing with: learning to play our parts and the like. I'm not rebelling. I'm just wondering my role in all of this.

Piddles.   You're Law. You stand for what is right and just.

Law.   I hope. But I'm seriously considering changing my name.

Agatha.   Can you do that?

Hatch.   Can *we* do that?

Law.   I don't know. I'll have to go through the legal channels and find out, maybe contact the playwright himself. I just don't know if Law encompasses who I am anymore.

Montaño.   What are you thinking?

Law.   Instead of Law, maybe "Justice"

Michael.   Uh, okay.

Law.   I don't know. I may go through a transition period. Maybe you guys could get used to calling me "The Character Formally Known as Law"?

Montaño.   That whole thing? As your name?

Law.   Maybe?

Match.   That's princely.

Piddles.   Until you figure it out, can we just call you Law? We don't have much time. This is a one-act.

Law.   (*Sighs*) For now.

SM.   I knew actors were crazy, but are characters becoming emotionally unstable as well? We have a reluctant leader, an overemotional twin, and a lawyer with an identity crisis.

Man.   You know, you deserved that baseball.

Law.   As a character, I did come right from that short play to this very scene. I'm still reeling a bit from the sting. Just give me a few minutes.

Agatha.   Actors can be a bit emotional and sometimes irrational. Perhaps that's what makes them able to represent characters that face the same variety of strengths and weaknesses of being human. The instability of the characters themselves could very well be a symbol for the role actors play in giving themselves so completely to becoming the characters. Of course, I'm trying to understand the playwright, as a writer myself, you know.

SM.   Or serve as a mouthpiece for him.

Hatch.   (*Starts crying*) Ohhh.

Match.   (*Deep breath*) It's okay, Hatch. I'm right here.

Hatch.   It's not that. I was just thinking about what Agatha said.

Match.   She said a lot. As usual.

Hatch.   About actors taking on the weaknesses and flaws of the characters.

Agatha.   Are you upset as the actor or the character?

Hatch.   I'm not upset for me.

Match.   What's the deal, then?

Hatch.   Just thinking about Heath Ledger.

Michael.   Whoa! No names.

Montaño.   (*As the Joker from* The Dark Knight) Why so serious?

Piddles.   Montaño, let's not.

Man.   I like this troupe.

SM.   I don't.

Montaño.   That's because you're an . . . (*looks out over the audience, hesitates, wants to say it but edits himself*) you're an . . . you're a . . . donkey.

SM.   Your sticks and stones are weak.

Montaño lunges toward SM, but Michael and Match stop him.

36

Montaño.   I'll cram sticks and stones where the sun don't shine.

Michael.   (*Loudly*) We have a task! We are characters given a duty! And we WILL perform that duty. (*to SM*) Stop being antagonistic!

SM.   Me?

Michael.   Yes, you. We all get along. You're the poison in the soup.

SM.   Perhaps that's because I'm the only one here focused enough to . . .

Michael.   Enough! You're crossing a line. I've seen actors replaced for years. Characters are a different story.

SM.   What are you saying?

Montaño.   (*Sneering*) You know what happens to problematic characters.

SM.   I'm a creation of this playwright just like you are.

Michael.   (*Making the point that SM had better be careful*) Exactly.

Agatha.   (*Reiterating Michael's point*) Exactly.

Piddles.   (*Reiterating Michael's point*) Exactly.

SM.   This isn't fair. You've been in the Beebles' universe longer.

Man.   *I* haven't.

SM.   (*Frustrated.*) I'm the way I was made. This is who I am.

Montaño.   Look who's emotional now!

SM.   This is who I was *written* to be.

Match.   Here we go again.

Piddles.   Michael, we have work to do.

Michael.   You're right. Go!

Piddles.   Half circle. Greek chorus.

Everyone scrambles to create a half circle with Piddles in the focus of the parabola. SM is slow-to-move.

Montaño.   She said move!

SM moves into place.

Piddles.   Stronger than lover's love is lover's hate. Incurable, in each, the wounds they make. (*pause*) Hate is a bottomless cup; I will pour and pour.

Law.   Wait. Is this . . . ?

37

Piddles. I know indeed what evil I intend to do, but stronger than all my afterthoughts is my fury, fury that brings upon mortals the greatest evils.

Law. Wait. There's no law or justice in this play.

Michael. It's a play, for goodness sake. Go with it.

Piddles. I understand too well the dreadful act I'm going to commit, but my judgement can't check my anger, and that incites the greatest evils human beings do.

Montaño. Piddles, I'm sorry. I can't do this.

Law. I can't either.

Michael. What are you doing?

Montaño. I'm sorry. I hate this play. "Medea" freaks me out! It's so cold, so cruel. I'm talking her and Jason both. I just can't.

Agatha. It's so perfect. You're an idealist.

SM. I don't suppose I'm allowed an opinion.

Michael. (*ignoring him*) I'm so sorry, Piddles. This isn't fair to you. This role . . .

Piddles. I hate it.

Michael. What?

Piddles. I hate it. I never wanted to play Medea. I'm more of a Brechtian, Williamsy, Becket-like, Shawite modern woman.

Michael. (*looks at her with admiration*) You know your stuff.

Piddles. I do. In fact . . .

She rushes to whisper in Montaño's ear. He smiles and nods.

Montaño. Sure!

Michael. What?

Piddles. You'll see. Hide behind the set. All of you, except Montaño.

They cautiously move behind the set. SM is the slowest.

Piddles. Move it, SM.

Montaño. (*in an Irish dialect, moving DR*) When I cast my mind back to that summer of 1936, different kinds of memories offer themselves to me. We got our first wireless set that summer. Well, a sort of a set, and it obsessed us. It arrived as August was about to begin. In the old days, August the first was La Lughnasa, and

38

the days and weeks of harvesting that followed were called the Festival of Lughnasa.

At the end of his lines, Montaño, remains standing DR and becomes Michael's "mirror."

Match.   Are we cross-gender acting?

Piddles.   Yes!

Match, Hatch, Piddles, and Michael enter as sisters and begin to pantomime the opening actions of "Dancing at Lughnasa" and they busy themselves with their tasks. PIDDLES (as MAGGIE) makes a mash for hens. MATCH (as AGNES) knits gloves. HATCH (as ROSE) carries a basket of turf into the kitchen and empties it into the large box beside the range. MICHAEL (as CHRIS) irons at the kitchen table. They all work in silence. Then CHRIS stops ironing, goes to the tiny mirror on the wall and scrutinizes her face.

Michael.   (*Looking in the 'mirror'— Montaño, who doesn't respond*) When are we going to get a decent mirror to see ourselves in?

Piddles.   You can see enough to do you.

Michael.   I'm going to throw this aul cracked thing out.

Piddles.   Indeed you're not, Chrissie. I'm the one that broke it and the only way to avoid seven years bad luck is to keep on using it.

Michael.   You can see nothing in it.

Match.   Except more and more wrinkles.

Michael.   D'you know what I think I might do? I think I just might start wearing lipstick.

Match.   Do you hear this, Maggie?

Piddles.   Steady on, girl. Today it's lipstick; tomorrow it's the gin bottle.

Work continues. Nobody speaks. Then suddenly and unexpectedly Hatch bursts into raucous song.

Hatch.   'Will you come to Abyssinia, will you come? Bring your own cup and saucer and a bun...'

As he sings the next two lines he dances – a gauche, graceless shuffle that defies the rhythm of the song.

Hatch.   'Mussolini will be there with his airplanes in the air, Will you come to Abyssinia, will you come?   Not bad, Maggie – eh?

Piddles tries to light a very short cigarette butt.

Piddles.   You should be on the stage, Rose.

Law (as Kate) enters. Everyone gets quiet.

Law.   Why do all of you look so happy? This is supposed to be an Irish family in an Irish play!

Radio music begins playing.

Law.   What's that ungodly noise?

Michael.   It's called music, Kate. Instruments. Chords.

Michael, Piddles, Match, and Hatch all shake and quiver from wanting to dance, but show self-restraint as they look at Law.

Finally, Match, as Agnes, speaks with intensity.

Match.   How many years has it been since we were at the harvest dance? - at any dance? And I don't care how young they are, how drunk and dirty and sweaty they are. I want to dance, Kate. It's the festival of Lughnasa. I'm only thirty-five. I want to dance.

Michael, Piddles, Match, and Hatch break out into crazy dance. Law looks at them, controlling his anger.

Law taps his foot, looks down at it, and purposefully stops it from tapping.

Agatha goes to Law.

Agatha.   (*Loudly, over the music*) Isn't this the part in Lughnasa where Kate gives in and dances with her sisters? Isn't that what you're supposed to do?

The music abruptly stops as Michael, Piddles, Match, and Hatch stop dancing at stare at Agatha. She has ruined the scene and the momentum of what was about to happen. Law, oblivious, flings his head back, in the silence, and omits a loud "Yaaah" as he begins to dance, very badly. Everyone stares at him. After six or seven seconds, he stops, out of breath and stares at everyone.

Law.   What?

Piddles.   Agatha ruined the moment.

Agatha.   Me?

Piddles.   Yes. He was about to join us.

Agatha.   But . . .

Piddles.   But you blared it out to the audience.

Hatch.   (*to Law*) Your dancing was really bad anyway.

Law.   I never claimed to be a dancer. I'm an officer of the . . . law.

SM.   Well, that was a failure.

Michael.   That's enough.

Man.   You guys are better than I thought. That was a good scene.

Piddles.   Until it was ruined. (*looks at Agatha*)

Agatha.   It's my job to state the obvious. It's like . . . foreshadowing.

Piddles.   There's a difference between foreshadowing and trolling.

Agatha.   Trolling? We're not online.

Piddles.   But we're onstage.

SM.   This is insane. How did I get written into this disaster?

Montaño.   (*upset with SM*) Michael!

Michael.   Just act!

Montaño begins to run around wailing as if he's the early version of Helen Keller from "The Miracle Worker." The other characters step back. Eventually Piddles goes up to Montaño and calms him. She begins forming sign letters with her fingers and putting them into his hand. He seems to understand for a second, then runs off wild again.

Michael.   (*As Captain Arthur Keller*) Young lady! You must convince me that there's the slightest hope of you teaching a child who now flees from you like the plague.

Piddles.   (*as Annie Sullivan*) There isn't. It's hopeless here.

SM.   Hopeless. (*The other actors glare at him.*)

Michael.   Am I to understand . . . ?

Piddles.   We all agree it's hopeless here. The next question is . . .

SM.   Why are you doing this?

Match, very upset, goes to sit far downstage.

Hatch follows him to comfort him.

Michael.   (*to SM*) I think it's time that you go.

SM.   Just disappear?

Law.   Your presence *is* rather damaging.

Piddles.   Why is it that there is always, *always* one character or one actor that can ruin everything for the rest of the group? It never fails.

SM.   Well, I can't just leave. I'm here. You should know how things work.

41

Man.   Oeeeeeeeeeedipus!!

Michael.   What?

Man.   Oeeeeeeeeeeedipus!!

Piddles.   Really?

Law.   Wait.

Agatha.   Are we doing this again?

Hatch.   Doing what? I'm confused.

Match.   See!

Piddles.   Going off-script again.   Oedipus is not in this script. I don't like Greek tragedies.
              I would have remembered.

Michael.   Is there some reason . . . ?

Montaño.   (*entering*) Greetings! Or should I say WOE!?!

Piddles.   Montaño, what are you doing?

Montaño.   I'm not Montaño. I'm the Oracle of Delphi.

Michael.   Montaño, this is not . . .

Montaño.   Trust me. Okay?

Michael.   (*sighs*) Okay.

Montaño.   I am the Oracle of Delphi.   And this (*motions off-stage*) is . . . (*a man in a mask
              enters*) Oedipus.

Piddles.   Who's that?

Faux Oedipus (FO).   I'm Oedipus.

Hatch.   No, really? Who are you?

Montaño.   He is Oedipus. And I have a prophecy for him!

Match.   Great.

Montaño.   And you (*points to SM*) are Laius, the father of Oedipus.

SM.   Wait a minute here.

Montaño.   And you (*to Piddles*) are Jocasta, the mother of Oedipus.

Piddles.   Ewwww.

SM.   I'm not doing this anymore. (*Moves to the top of the set and crosses his arms.*)

42

Piddles. I don't know any of these lines.

Montaño. You don't need to. Oedipus. Echo me on that part, Man.

Man. Okay.

Montaño. Oedipus!

Man. Oeeeeeeeeeeeedipus!

Montaño. Know this, your fate. You shall kill your father and marry your mother.

Piddles. This is why I hate Greek plays.

SM. Wait a minute.

FO. No! I shall not allow this fate.

Michael. I know that voice.

FO. I shall cross the entirety of Greece to run from this prophecy.

FO runs in circles and ends up at the set.

FO. Move, old man. You are in my way.

SM. I'm not playing this game.

FO. I said move from this narrow path on the edge of this high mountain so that I can continue. I shall say please just once.

SM. I'm not doing this.

FO. You won't move.

SM. No, I won't act anymore. I'm not playing Laius.

FO. Then I shall come by you anyway.

SM. Don't come up here.

FO goes to the top of the set and starts to shove SM.

SM. Stop. I'm not doing this.

FO. I'm just trying to get past you, old man.

SM. Stop. Seriously. Stop.

FO bumps into SM and then throws him off the highest part of the set, causing him to fall off the set. He lies lifeless. The character should slip off-stage and prepare for his dramatic reentrance.

Piddles. Wait. What just happened?

FO turns and faces the audience. His arms are crossed.

Michael.   Hey. (*walking toward SM*) Hey!

Montaño.   He can't hear you.

Hatch.   What?

Match.   (*Getting up*) What?

Agatha.   (*Excited*) Is this what I think this is?

Michael.   He can't. He's "The Stage Manager."

Montaño.   Well . . .

Michael.   (*to Faux Oedipus*) And who are you? You just . . . You didn't . . .

The Grim Reaper enters.

Grim.   Am I in the right place?

Montaño.   Yes. I heard you were coming!

Piddles.   What's going on? Are you . . . ?

Grim.   Probably. The outfit gives it away, right?

Michael.   Are you saying that SM . . . ? And you're the . . . ?

Grim.   Well, I started out a long, long time ago. I don't really remember when. I've been doing my business for a few millennia. A few hundred years back, a couple of brothers tried to steal my name, starting telling tales of my business and all. I took care of them, and I take care of people now. I must say that it's been a while since I've been on a real stage. I did a bit of acting back in high school, but that was long before plays were a thing. But to be called on a stage to get a real character is a treat.

Michael.   He's dead. Not pretend dead? Not fake dead? Dead.

Montaño.   Dead.

Michael.   (*to Montaño*) What'd you do?

Montaño.   Not much. I was, you know, Helen Keller, all, uggh and waah and blah-do-blah and there was Faux Oedipus standing there in his mask. I was all, "Whoa. Wait a minute. This isn't part of the show." Then he told me who was and that—are you ready for this—the playwright sent him to come and get rid SM, in character, in scene.

Michael.   What?

Montaño.   The guy wasn't doing his job. He was counterproductive. You know it.

44

Hatch. That's true.

Agatha. That is true.

Montaño. His character didn't fit in with the rest of the show. And since he is a character, you know, . . .

Piddles. The playwright wrote him out.

Montaño. Exactly.

Law. Whoa.

Michael. (*to Faux Oedipus*) But who are you?

Montaño. He was brought back to help us out.

Piddles. Brought back?

FO removes his mask to reveal Brannon from the previous Beebles play.

Everyone. Brannon!!

Everyone except Michael, Montaño, and Man gathers around Brannon to hug him.

Michael. Brought him back?

Montaño. Well, the playwright can do whatever he wants, right?

FO. Hello, everyone. Careful. Careful. Newly alive here.

Piddles. You're alive!

FO. Yes, I seem to be. I have a tendency to die quite a bit. This time the resurrection was a bit abrupt.

Hatch. It's so good to see you, sir!

Man. This is the famous Brannon?

FO. And this is?

Hatch. This is the man.

FO. The man?

Piddles. An actor in this show

FO. If I may ask a favor, could you all refrain from calling me Brannon? That name has a deathly stigma for me. Please call me FO from now on, for Faux Oedipus. It's not the most pleasant name in the world, but neither is Brannon anymore, and well, we're on the stage. FO for Faux Oedipus.

Michael. Really?

FO.   Really.

Piddles.   We can do that. *(She hugs him.)*

FO.   Please. Please. Okay. Thanks.

Grim.   Can I please do my job?

Piddles.   Of course, I guess.

Grim.   I mean, I'm trying here. It's not a fun task. Seriously. And this stage thing freaks me out a bit. The last time I was on stage, it was supposedly in Swindon, England, but I doubt I was really there. And they told me it was 1998, but it couldn't be. I guess it *could* be 1998 during the actual play. I just show up where you all need me. It was for some dog named Wellington that had been stabbed with some sort of garden utensil. A kid named Christopher, excuse me, *(British accent) ChristahFUH*, was freaking out and wailing. Well, I guess he was a kid. He was, according to him, 15 years, 3 months, and 2 days old. It was odd. And it was on stage, which caught me off guard.

Montaño.   What a curious incident!

Hatch.   And it was about a dog?

Match.   In the night-time?

Michael.   *(to Grim)* Are you who you say you are?

Grim.   Unfortunately. *(Beat)* And there's a dead body over there.

Michael.   Can "The Stage Manager" actually die?

Law.   If it's written in the script

Michael.   Well, yeah. I guess.

Grim.   You may not like it, but I'm here.

Hatch.   And we're down an actor.

Agatha.   We are. But we've covered quite a few plays.

FO.   You've referenced several shows already then?

Michael.   We have.

FO.   I respect that. Could you use some help in doing some more?

Piddles.   Would you?

FO.   Sure. Why not? I'm here.

Grim.   Is no one going to ask me?

46

Michael.   What?

Grim.   I'm on stage. That dead guy's not going anywhere.

Michael.   (*looking out over the audience*) Our playwright's a strange man, strange.

Montaño.   But he fixed our problem.

Match.   By killing someone!

Hatch.   A character.

Piddles.   (*to Grim*) You want to act?

Grim.   I'm well-known for my job, but as an actor, I'm pretty much a dark horse.

Montaño.   (*Excited, stepping forward*) A dark horse?

Piddles.   What?

Montaño.   A horse?! Horses? They saw me. They saw what I did. They saw my sin.

Michael.   Montaño.

Montaño.   A young man. Horses. A crime. Must find the reason.

Montaño starts pulling off some clothes. He pulls off his shirt, runs to the top of the set and pulls off his shoes and socks. Before he stops, he has unbuttoned his pants, but he has NOT pulled them down.

During this whole time, Michael, Law, FO, and Piddles are screaming for him to stop.

Piddles.   Montaño!

Michael.   No, Montaño. You can't do that!

Law.   We can't do "Equus" on this stage!

FO.   Montaño, keep your clothes on! For goodness sake!

Montaño stops.

Montaño.   All you ever do is stop me.

Match.   All you ever do is strip.

Montaño.   "Equus" is a Tony-Award-winning play

Michael.   That we can't do in this show

Match.   You're pretty bad about going to extremes.

FO.   Please put your shirt back on.

Montaño puts his shirt back on, but does not put his socks and shoes back on.

47

Montaño.   You're no fun.

Agatha.   I thought it was fun.

Grim.   You ought to see some of the things I've seen. Nothing would shock you. People are crazy. I mean crazy.

FO.   Michael, this is "The Beebles Refrain," right?

Michael.   I think so. Yes. Unless I've lost my mind, yes.

FO.   And that means . . . ?

Michael.   We are here, all of us, as a result of our original connection with Beebles.

Man.   Except for me.

Piddles.   But you're one of us now.

Hatch.   Yeah, you are.

Man.   I am?

Piddles.   Of course.

Michael.   And when we're on this stage, we are living out the vision of what we learned during our unity, our accord. We are characters playing characters. Actors are our characters playing our characters for the sake of characters.

Match.   My head hurts.

FO.   And, Michael, you've got it. Yes, sir!

Michael.   We don't age. We stay who we are.

FO.   Because on this stage, time is not an issue.

Michael.   No matter how many times we perform this play, our characters will . . .

Piddles.   Still be the same. Oh!

Montaño.   Wait. That's the testament about time. That art is the enemy . . .

Michael.   Of TIME.

Hatch.   Oh.

Man.   This whole experience is pretty awesome. On this stage.

Piddles.   On this stage, you guys.

Everyone.   On this stage. (*Left foot stomp, right foot stomp twice, left foot stomp*)

Piddles.   That's what I'm talking about.

Match.   Wait a minute. Are we eternal?

Law.   As characters. Yes. Forever in the script. Forever in the memory.

Match.   Oh, it's starting to make sense.

Michael.   And we do have the power of creation, to make new things and new experiences, we also bring what we have to that which is already engraved into the art of humanity.

FO.   That's what I've figured out. And it took dying a few times for me to get it. You're ahead of the game.

Michael.   And we are as strong as our lines

FO.   And our ability to deliver them well.

Michael.   So, Aunt Martha, Aunt Abby, how did he die?

Agatha and Piddles run up to assume the roles of Aunt Martha and Aunt Abby.

Agatha.   Oh, Mortimer, don't be so inquisitive. The gentleman died because he drank some wine with poison in it.

Michael.   Well, how did the poison get in the wine?

Piddles.   Well, we put it in wine because it's less noticeable. When it's in tea it has a distinct odor.

Law.   Bravo!

Hatch.   I love that play!

Michael.   Take this. (*Throws him a long, fake nose.*) You know what to do.

Hatch.   Seriously?

Michael.   Go for it.

Hatch.   (*as Cyrano*) A great nose may be an index of a great soul!

Match.   Oh, my friend, can you help me win the love of Roxanne?

Montaño.   (*starts singing "Roxanne" from the Police/"Moulin Rouge"*) ROXANNE!

Michael.   No. Not here. This is the original.

Montaño.   Cyrano! Are you okay?

Hatch.   I'm not well.

Match.   Looking for love in all the wrong places.

Michael.   You stop, too.

Hatch.   A lifetime later, and I still was unable to tell the woman I love that I love her.

Hatch gets weaker and weaker and starts to die.

Agatha.   (*as Roxanne*) All those letters, they were you. All those beautiful powerful words, they were you! The voice from the shadows, that was you. You always loved me!

Piddles.   (*singing*) And I-I-I will always love you, I-I will always love you!

Michael.   Piddles!

Law.   Copyright!

Agatha.   Live, for I love you!

Hatch.   No, in fairy tales when to the ill-starred prince the lady says 'I love you,' all his ugliness fades fast—but I remain the same, up to the last!

Agatha.   I have marred your life. I, I . . .

Hatch.   You blessed my life! Never on me had rested woman's love. My mother even could not find me fair: I had no sister; and, when grown a man, I feared the mistress who would mock at me. But I have had your friendship—grace to you. A woman's charm has passed across my path.

Hatch dies.

Agatha cries.

Piddles, Match, Man, Grim, and Law clap.

Piddles.   That was beautiful, just beautiful.

FO.   Well done.

Piddles.   Are you alive?

Hatch.   Yeah, I'm here.

Grim.   Good. I don't like two at once. Messy. And it's a muscle strain.

Michael.   (*tossing Grim a set of keys*) Here. Give it a shot.

Grim.   Me? Really?

Michael.   Yeah, you. He wrote you in this play for some reason.

Grim.   But you know what my field of expertise is.

Michael.   Why do you think I tossed you the keys?

Grim.   (*realizing what they mean*) Oooh!

Michael.   Yeah.

Piddles.   (*to Michael*) His field of expertise is . . . death.

Michael.   Exactly.

Grim.   I tell you, boys, and you listen to me, boys. Learn this lesson. Be liked and you will never want. You take me, for instance. I never have to wait in line to see a buyer. 'Willy Loman is here!' That's all they have to know, and I go right through."   That's the life of a salesman, I tell you. And one of the greatest men I ever knew, he died the death of a salesman, in his green velvet slippers in the smoker of the New York, New Haven, and Hartford, going into Boston—when he died, hundreds of salesmen and buyers were at the funeral. That's a successful life. That's a beloved man.

Montaño.   (*Signing to the tune of "Honesty"*) Irony is just such a lonely word.

Match.   That's impressive.

Montaño.   Thank you.

Match.   I was talking to Grim.

Agatha.   Burn!

Law.   And then BOOM.

Agatha.   What?

Law.   And then BOOM. In the play. Not your "burn." After Willy Loman's speeches, he takes his keys and then BOOM.

Grim.   And then I'd be called. To the stage. Again.

FO.   Called to the stage.

Michael.   You caught that, too?

Piddles.   (*looking around*) Called to the stage.

Match.   But what if it doesn't turn out right? Or if we're not as perfect as we need to be?

Hatch.   It doesn't matter.

Law.   It doesn't matter.

Man.   The show must go on.

Agatha.   The show must go on.

Michael.   The show must go on.

Piddles.   (*Quoting Queen's song, with the song's rhythm*) Inside my heart is breaking, my make-up may be flaking, but my smile still stays on.

Montaño.   Go on!

Michael.   Two households, both alike in dignity,

             In fair Verona, where we lay our scene,

             From ancient grudge break to new mutiny,

             Where civil blood makes civil hands unclean.

Man.   Oh! I know this one.

Montaño runs up to and climbs the ladder.

Montaño.   Romeo!

Piddles.   Wait!

Montaño.   What?

Piddles.   Are you playing Juliet?

Montaño.   Sure. Why not?

Piddles.   Because . . . what do *I* play? Romeo?

Montaño.   Sure. Why not? Be the Romeo you want to see in the world!

Law.   Do you bite your tongue at us, sir?

Michael.   Good. Keep it going.

Piddles.   But, soft, what light through yonder window breaks?

             It is the east, and Juliet is the sun.

Match.   That which we call a rose

             By any other word would smell as sweet.

Montaño.   Aren't I Juliet? What are you doing?

Match.   Being the *Juliet* I want to see in the world.

FO.   A plague o' both your houses!

Michael.   Romeo, Romeo, Romeo! Here's drink: I drink to thee.

Agatha.   Parting is such sweet sorrow.

Montaño.   (*Quickly and dramatically*) O happy dagger,

             This is thy sheath: there rust, and let me die.

Hatch.   All are punished.

Michael.   For never was a story of more woe

            Than this of Juliet and her Romeo.

Piddles.   Bravo!

Law.   I didn't realize that was actually in the script. It just flowed, though.

Montaño.   It's the transition to . . .

The lights flash and loud Polka music begins.

Michael.   (*yelling*) No. Wrong music.

The music stops.

Montaño.   It's the transition to . . .

The lights flash and loud hip-hop music begins.

Michael.   (*yelling*) No! No! That was the wrong music, too.

FO.   Track 14.

The lights flash and ominous, spooky music begins. The characters move to create a large, varied tableau across the stage.

Michael.   There you go. And here we go.

FO.   I am thy father's spirit,

            Doom'd for a certain term to walk the night.

            Revenge his foul and most unnatural murther.

Hatch.   Neither a borrower nor a lender be;
            For loan oft loses both itself and friend,
            and borrowing dulls the edge of husbandry.

Agatha.   This above all: to thine own self be true

Man.   And it must follow, as the night the day,
            thou canst not then be false to any man.

Match.   Wait. Be true?

Michael.   We're in *Hamlet*, Match.

Match.   I know that, but . . .

Montaño.   Doubt that the sun doth move, doubt truth to be a liar, but never doubt I love.

Match.   Doubt? Doubt that we love?

53

Piddles.   Are you all right, Match?

Match.   We've lost track of Beebles.

Law.   A little more than kin, and less than kind

Piddles.   She's with Colton. She's not here anymore. I understand that.

Agatha.   This is the very ecstasy of love.

Match.   But it's more than that. Beebles is what we look for, what we strive for.

Grim.   Though this be madness, yet there is method in 't.

Piddles.   Oh, Match. I know. I know. We know Beebles. She was such a part of making us good. She kept us going.

Man.   The lady doth protest too much, methinks.

Michael.   Match, you're having misgivings. You're still struggling. I understand.

FO.   When sorrows come, they come not single spies, but in battalions.

Match.   Beebles is important, but she's even more important because she helped us realize why we do what we do.

Piddles.   Because we could look at her and see goodness . . . and innocence

Montaño.   To be, or not to be: that is the question. Whether 'tis nobler in the mind to suffer the slings and arrows of outrageous fortune . . .

Michael.   And she helped us to see what we could be if we stopped focusing on ourselves.

Montaño.   . . . and by opposing, end them.

Michael.   We're characters and we're here a short time.

Man.   The play's the thing wherein I'll catch the conscience of the king

Michael.   The play's the thing.

Piddles.   The play's the thing.

Match.   The play's the thing.

FO.   This play.

Hatch.   This play?

FO.   This play. You're characters. One and all. What is your role? And what is your responsibility?

Agatha.   To the script

Man.   And to the play

Michael.	To be faithful while we're here
FO.	So, Grim. What's your decision?
Piddles.	What decision?
Grim.	Obviously, this one. (*He moves his arm toward SM*)
SM.	(*Standing up*) What a piece of work is man! How noble in reason! How infinite in faculty! In form and moving how express and admirable! in action how like an angel! In apprehension how like a god! The beauty of the world, the paragon of animals!
Montaño.	What?
Agatha.	SM?
Man.	How?
Michael.	He was . . . (*looks at FO, then at SM*) Wait. Who are you?
Piddles.	Was he dead?
FO.	Oh, yes. Very dead.
SM.	But I'm here. Very much here.
Hatch.	But, Michael, you said "The Stage Manager" couldn't die, but then he did, but now he's not. I'm confused.
Match.	Wait a minute.
Agatha.	This is a reverse of what I normally deal with.
Michael.	If he was written as dead, how could you just bring him back?
Piddles.	You brought him back?
Grim.	Well, this show is a comedy, ultimately. You just can't have people arbitrarily dying, you know, with all the sorrow and unresolved pain.
FO.	And a wise decision it was.
SM.	And I thank you. I have a bit more clarity of thought now.
FO.	(*to SM*) Isn't *that* the truth? The third time's the charm, though.
Michael.	I'm trying to make sense of this.
Match.	(*to Grim*) Are you? And that makes us . . . ?
Grim.	(*Walking around, looking at everyone*) You are so special. You get to live forever. You get to live forever. Look around you. This stage, these lights, this floor, this experience. If the paper you're written on is burned, if the files

containing your lines are lost or erased, if the video recording, legal or illegal, is destroyed, you are *still* immortal because you lived and walked on this stage. Humans live, age, and die, but the essence who they are lives on because *you* live. You are here now. Soon, this performance will be memory, but it's forever etched in time. Humanity preserves the best and strongest of what we are in art. Here. On this stage, in a song, on a canvas, in a block of marble, and in the memory of those who are open to it.

Match.   So, I'm right.

FO.   You're right.

Michael.   Wait. You're the playwright?

Piddles.   The playwright?

FO.   And our roles, our job as characters is just as important in a play about our beloved cow as it is about any other adventure story ever told.

Michael.   You made all this. You wrote us.

Grim.   I'm just a writer.

Piddles.   And not just the keeper of death, but of life on this stage.

Grim.   I type what you become. I record your journey as it happens.

Match.   We know our tasks, but even for the best of us, it can get overwhelming and frustrating.

Grim.   But the same is true of humanity. We know our task, but even for the *best* of us, it can get overwhelming and frustrating. But that's why we need you. By exploring what you do and who you become, we get to examine ourselves and our motives.

Man.   Is that why we're here?

Grim.   You are that which reflects the best of us.

Law.   Is that really true?

Grim.   Yes. You are that which reflects the best of us.

Michael.   (*to FO*) And you knew?

FO.   Well, I mentioned in the last play that I knew the playwright.

Montaño.   So, this is still real? We're still in the show?

Grim.   We are.

Montaño.   (*looking out over the audience*) But what if no one comes to watch the show?

Grim.   That's a possibility.

56

Piddles.   And what if people don't like it?

Grim.   That's a big possibility as well.

Law.   You mean some people may feel forced to watch it?

Grim.   That happens. Family. Contests.

Michael.   But our families are out there. Genetics or not. I can feel that this place is filled with family.

Grim.   More than you realize. (*moves down left to watch the end of the show*) But there's something else you need to realize.

Grim remains DL for the rest of the show.

Michael.   What's that?

The characters move themselves into a line at the front of the stage, facing the audience.

FO.   This *stage* is filled with family.

Hatch.   The characters

Match.   Here for just a short moment in time

Agatha .   The actors portraying the characters

Man.   Becoming who they need to be in order to be faithful to the script

Law.   The light technicians

SM.   And sound technicians

Piddles.   And the backstage crew

Michael.   And yes, all the people who support those *on* this stage

FO.   Working together, even when they don't understand

As the following line is spoken, each character pulls out thumb lines and lift them into the air on the word "theatre."

The image on the cyc changes to a face of a clock. As various lines are spoken, each character, one at a time, on a predetermined line "throws" his or her light at the clock on the cyc, releasing the characters' energy to the show, to the time, to the art. As each person throws, the clock changes colors, until the last person has thrown his light. As they throw, they each take a seat on the upstage set.

Montaño.   Creating this beautiful, powerful thing called theatre

Piddles.   And we, as characters,

Agatha.   Play our parts

57

Hatch.   Whether it's in time-tested classics

Match.   Or in newer works

Michael.   Or in creating some totally fresh in both draft and final form

Piddles.   To understand

Man.   To appreciate

SM.   To celebrate

FO.   To proclaim that

ALL (*except Grim*)   This gift, this privilege to create

Piddles.   Is a duty and function

FO.   Of time

Hatch.   Time

Michael.   Time

Agatha.   And of art.

SM.   Art

Man.   Art

Michael.   Together in one moment, at one place, here

ALL (*except Grim*) On this stage.

Grim.   This stage.

ALL.   This stage.

Grim.   This moment.

ALL.   This moment.

Grim.   This fleeting moment

Michael.   That will never return.

Piddles.   (*Standing*) Never.

Michael.   (*Standing*) But will forever be. (*On the word "be," he motions toward the clock image on the cyc. Upon his movement, the clock image shatters, breaking the illusion of time on art.*)

Piddles.   Forever.

FO.   Forever.

Match.   Forever.

Grim.   And so, Stage Manager . . .

From the upstage set, the actors, other than Grim, watch SM.

SM.   (*Stepping up*) Well, it's getting late here on this stage, at least for this play. We're
            to the end of the script for "The Beebles Refrain," a coming together *again* to
            figure out why we're here and what we're doing. But once again, I think we just
            might have figured it out. We hope *you* have, too. If you haven't, there's not
            much we can do about that, now is there? So, to all of you we say "good luck."

Everybody except Grim gasps and runs up near SM.

Montaño.   You can't say that!

Montaño pulls out a baseball and throws it at SM, knocking him down and out.

ALL (*except Grim*).   Montaño!

Montaño.   I regret nothing.

The stage goes black.

ONE-ACT, UNDER-40-MINUTE VERSION
IF A ONE-ACT VERSION OF THIS PLAY IS PERFORMED, THE FOLLOWING
CUTTING, OMITTING THE PARTS THAT HAVE THE "STRIKETHROUGH," MUST
BE USED.

The Beebles Refrain,
Another Testament of Time and Art

In the darkness, ominous music starts playing. A blue light gradually rises. Fog fills the air.
There is a loud knocking. Five knocks. There is a pause. Five more knocks. The sound of a
man's voice BEGINNING off stage.

Man.   (*Entering, speaking with a Scottish brogue*) Knock, knock, knock! Who's there, i'
             the name of Beelzebub? ~~Here's a farmer that hanged himself on the expectation of~~
             ~~plenty.~~

The knocking continues.

Man.   Knock, knock! Who's there, in the other devil's name?

Knocking within

Man.   Knock, knock, knock! Who's there? ~~Faith, here's an English tailor come hither, for~~
             ~~stealing out of a French hose~~: come in, tailor; here you may
             roast your goose.

~~*Knocking within*~~

~~Man.   Knock, knock; never at quiet! What are you? But this place is too cold for hell.~~

The man opens the gate. Another man, THE STAGE MANAGER, walks in. He is backlit.

SM.   This play is called "The Beebles Refrain, Another Testament of Time and Art.'

Man.   Who are you?

SM.   You know who it's written, produced, and directed by. You should have
             programs. (*Looks around*) The name of this place is Dunsinane, Scotland, as you
             may have figured out, just north of Hadrian's Wall, the latitude and the longitude
             uncertain, since, of course, it's fictitious.

Man.   Fictitious?

SM.   This one-act is a parody. Just like the original "Beebles ACCORD," it contains
               all kinds of theatre and play references that most people don't catch—as we've
               learned, even people who should catch them sometimes don't. This particular play
               is called "M . . ."

Man.   No! Are ye mad an' off yer bonkers, ye crazy man, ye?

SM.   What?

Man.   Ye c'nno' say the name of the play. You're supposed to call it "The
               Sco'ish Play."

SM.   First, there are many Scottish plays. Second, I don't believe in silly superstitions.
               And last, we're currently in the actual play. Even if people adhere to crazy ways,
               you're allowed to use the name during the performance.

Man.   Is that a fact?

SM.   I'm the Stage Manager. I know these things.

Man.   The Stage Ma'ager?

SM.   The Stage Manager. Created by Thornton Wilder. 1901. Grover's Corners. The
               Stage Manager.

Man.   Oh.

SM.   Yes.

Man.   Well, I defer to you.

SM.   Where was I?

Man.   Discussing Dunsinane.

SM.   I don't think that's right.

Man.   Aye. It *was* right; you were talking about this great castle.

SM.   Are you sure? I was certain I was talking about something verboten and taboo. I
               just can't remember. You've disturbed my internal vibrations.

Man.   Your what? And speak English, would you! Don't use none of those fancy stage-
               manager words on me.

SM.   May I please continue?

Man.   Nobody's stoppin' ye.

SM.   Ah, yes. I remember. The *play* references throughout this script! This particular
               script is one that most audiences are aware of, from the witches' brew to Burnham

Wood, from the ghost of Banquo to the unwashable spot, we start with one of Shakespeare's master works, "The Tragedy of . . ."

Man.   You're going to tempt fate again?

SM.   "Macbeth."

The Man looks around, as if anticipating death or for one of its lesser brothers to appear.

The SM looks around defiantly.

SM.   What are you doing? There's nothing happening.   I'm standing here.

The Man pokes the SM's arm from a distance.

SM.   See. I'm still here. There is no curse.

Out of nowhere, a baseball comes and hits the SM, causing him to fall out as if dead.

Man.   (wide-eyed) Ooooooooooooooooooooooh. I told ye so! You be dancin' on ye mum's grave with that kind of rebellion. (*looks around, then bends down to whisper loudly to SM*) Don't say I did't warn ye! (*Beat*) Do you be being alive? ~~Listen there, lad! Are you being alive? Did someone hold you too close? Did someone hurt you too deep?~~ Ye catch that reference, Neil Patrick?

Montaño.   Anybody seen my ball? Wait, is this . . . ? The show hasn't begun yet, has it?

Man.   Ay, there was already the knocking at the gate, and this poor unfortunate soul wantin' to be where the people are and callin' himself the Stage Manager came in and started talking all his gobbledy gook.

Montaño looks at the SM.

Montaño.   The Stage Manager? What? ~~What's wrong with him?~~ He looks . . .

Man.   He was talkin' and talkin' and actually said the *real* name of the Sco'ish play, the name that shall not be named, the cursed title of the Voldemort of Shakespeare. Then this white thing came out of nowhere and hit him. Down he went.

Montaño.   My ball hit him?

~~Man.   Was that wha' it was? Oh. Sounds like a personal problem to me.~~

Montaño.   Oh, man. It's not . . . No, it's not . . . And the play *started* already? It wasn't supposed to . . .

Man.   I've told ye before. The show began. The Stage Manager here called it (*searching*) "The Beebles . . . Refrain" or somet'in' like that.

Montaño slowly looks out over the audience, realizing that there IS an audience.

62

Montaño.   Oh, man. Jiminy Cricket on a pogo stick! They're here and watching. (*yelling*)
            Guys! GUYS! Get out here quick! GUYS!!

Michael, Piddles, and Hatch come onto the stage, finishing putting on their costumes, putting a layer of giant furry cloaks on top of their nice, theatre attire.

Piddles.   What's wrong, Montaño? We're trying ~~to get these monstrosities on~~ to cover up
            our nice clothes, like we did with the Chalk Circle. These Scottish Play pieces are
            too ~~heavy, though.~~ I don't know if we even need them.

Michael.   What's going on? (*referring to the Stage Manager*) Who's he?

Montaño.   The Stage Manager. *The* Stage Manager.

Michael.   The Stage Manager? (*Beat*) From "Our . . ."

Montaño.   From our play.

Michael.   What's he doing like that?

Montaño.   (*subtly pointing to the audience*) Look out there.

Michael.   What?

Montaño.   Look. Out. There.

Piddles.   What are *they* doing out there?

Montaño.   The play already started several minutes ago.

Michael.   What?

Hatch.   It what?

Man.   ~~He started knocking. I had to go and open it. These people were waiting. The
            eerie music and stage lighting had already begun as well.~~ That person in black
            back there pointed at me and said it was my cue.

~~Michael.~~   ~~(*Referring to The Stage Manager*) What's wrong with him?~~

Piddles.   Michael, we have to join the show in progress.

Michael.   What *happened* to him?

~~Piddles.~~   ~~(*looking out over the audience*) Michael, we have to start acting. It's already
            started.~~

Montaño.   I think I accidently hit him with my baseball.

Michael.   What?

Piddles.   Oh, Montaño! Have you already killed someone?

Hatch. ~~The horror.~~

Montaño. Does that mean . . . ?

Piddles. I'm afraid so.

Hatch. ~~So, we're expecting . . . ?~~

Michael. ~~And so early in the script.~~

Agatha enters.

Agatha. Do I sense a sense of resistance to my insistence to make an entrance?

Piddles. What?

Man. Is this woman a poet?

Agatha. Many have wondered. And many have rightfully been in awe. But I'm just a world-class writer, a novelist, a playwright, a solver of mysteries, a master of the enigmas presented by murder.

Michael. We know, Agatha. ~~We know who you are. It's us. And . . . you.~~

Piddles. We haven't seen you since Beebles showed up at the end of the last play.

Agatha. I know. We haven't been on stage since then.

Piddles. True. Come to think of it, that's the last time we were all together.

Michael. It's the last time we could be together. That's when our characters last saw each other. *But* I'm more concerned about the Stage Manager.

Agatha. Ooooh! Get ready for it. This man looks dead.

Michael. But he can't be.

Montaño. No, he can't be. Please don't be.

Piddles. Nobody blames you, Montaño. It was an accident.

Michael. You don't understand what I'm saying. He *can't* be dead. Haven't you read "Our Town"? He's immortal. The Stage Manager . . .

Agatha. Looks pretty dead to me.

Hatch. This isn't good.

Agatha. Oh, Hatch. Hello. Where's your twin?

Hatch. *(Lip quivering from being upset)* Match?

Agatha. Yes, Hatch. Where's Match?

Hatch. *(starts crying)* He left.

Agatha.   I'm sorry. I didn't mean to . . .

Piddles.   (*comforting Hatch*) It's just a touchy subject. Match just . . .

Hatch.   He went to find himself. He didn't want to be known as one half of "the twins."
            He wasn't content to be *Match*. He went to . . . (*sobbing*)

Agatha.   Where?

Piddles.   Buffalo.

Agatha.   New York?

Montaño.   No, Texas. He wanted to remake himself. Get a tan. There's a good sun over
            Buffalo.

Michael.   Can we focus on this man?

Man.   Me? Want to focus on me?

Michael.   What? No. The Stage Manager.

Man.   Because I'm the man, you know. That's my actual name. ~~Even in the script.~~
            ~~Probably in the "Beebles Refrain" text itself.~~ I'm the generic man who does
            what's needed for the scene, to help it along.

Hatch.   Wait. That's what my brother and I were. We were ~~the lackies, the aesthetic~~
            ~~element,~~ the sidekicks.

Man.   Well, evidently, you're no longer a team.

Hatch.   (*crying*) Match.

Piddles.   (*to Man*) Stop!

Man.   Can I become your brother?

Hatch.   What? No!

Man.   I'd really like a name.

Michael.   Can we please focus on the problem at hand? The clock is ticking.

Agatha.   (*Proclaiming*) This man is . . .

SM.   (*Getting up*) very much alive.

Everyone jumps back a bit.

Agatha.   Drat.

~~Piddles.   Here we go again.~~

Michael.   What's going on?

65

SM.   I was just lying there, listening to everything you've been saying.

Montaño.   You're alive! (H*e hugs the SM*)

SM.   (*Uncomfortable with the hug*) I'm the Stage Manager. I can't die. Now please get off of me.

Montaño releases him.

~~Michael.   That's what I said.~~

~~Piddles.   That's what he said. (*realizing that the "That's what she said" joke doesn't work with the he pronoun*) Oh, it doesn't work that way, does it?~~

~~Hatch.   No.~~

~~Michael.   Why? Why would you do that?~~

SM.   ~~Well,~~ I was ~~indeed~~ hit by a baseball, evidently from Montaño here.

Montaño.   Sorry.

SM.   It knocked the wind out of me. But when you all came up, I wanted to see what your intentions were, why you weren't already out on stage when the show started.

~~Michael.   You started it early.~~

~~SM.   I'm the Stage Manager.~~

Piddles.   We didn't have time to get all the cloaks on. You could have waited.

SM.   I'm the Stage Manager.

Man.   Are we going on with the Sco'ish play?

SM.   Yes.

Michael.   I'm the leader of this troupe now. This play, this script, this series of scripts— they're our home.

SM.   But I'm . . .

Michael.   Not the real stage manager. You're the character "The Stage Manager."

SM.   Don't confuse me. (*looking to the audience*) Or them.

Michael.   (*Takes a deep breath*) Places everyone. (*To the Stage Manager*) You, too.

Everyone builds a tableau, looking toward the Stage Manager, as he begins.

SM.   This play, this play within the parody, this referenced work . . .

Hatch.   We get it.

SM.   Is set in rural Scotland during dark ages of humanity's past.

We hear various farm animals bleating, neighing, etc.

SM.   A time in which . . .

Piddles.   Did I just hear Beebles?

Michael.   You couldn't have.

Hatch.   I thought I heard her, too.

Michael.   Beebles isn't here.

Agatha.   It sure sounded like her bellow to me, too.

Montaño.   (*to the audience*) For those of you who may not know or who may not remember, Beebles is a very special cow that was missing in "The Beebles Accord." At the end of the play, she returned to her owner, our friend, Colton, ~~even though a few original audience members didn't listen to all the cow references.~~

~~Michael.~~   ~~Montaño.~~

~~Montaño.~~   ~~A young man even said out loud after the standing ovation, "Oh! Beebles is a cow!"~~

Michael.   Montaño.

Montaño.   So, yeah, Beebles is a cow. Jus' sayin'. (*self-satisfied*) I'm finished.

SM.   May I please continue?

Michael.   Look, I'd like it to be her just as much as you. When I met her, I understood. She brings a certain peace. But she's not here.

Piddles.   This play *is* called "The Beebles *Refrain*." Doesn't that mean that there's a repetition?

Hatch.   Yeah.

Agatha.   That is the definition.

Michael.   (*to Hatch and Agatha*) You're getting her hopes up.

Agatha.   What are you talking about?

Michael.   (*pulling Agatha aside*) Colton. You do remember Colton? The one Piddles loved? The boy looking for his cow?

Agatha.   Yes, that *was* part of the premise of the first play.

Michael.   He found Beebles.

~~Agatha.~~   ~~I know. I was there.~~

67

Michael.   And then he ran off and married a super model named Amber.

Agatha.   What?

Michael.   He married a super model. He's living in Paris now.

Agatha.   Wait. I thought he . . .

Michael.   Wasn't interested in Piddles?

Agatha.   I thought he wasn't interested . . .

Michael.   . . . in Piddles.

Agatha.   Oh.

Hatch.   (*Walking up*) He did have a good sense of style, though.

Piddles.   Are you talking about me?

Michael.   (*taking leadership*) This play covers all new references.

Man.   Can I change roles now?

SM.   Not yet.

Michael.   New play.

SM.   But . . .

Michael.   New play.

Piddles.   You're taking this new leadership role seriously.

Michael.   That's my job. We bring words to life. We bring art to life. All that jazz. Right?

Piddles.   Sexy.

Michael.   And our job, yet again, is to present it all, the good and the bad, the uplifting, and the dark.

Michael hands a tunic to SM.

The others scramble for tunics.

Michael.   (*to SM, giving him his line*) The Ides of March are come.

SM.   Now?

Michael.   (*to SM, insistent*) The Ides of March are come.

SM.   (*sighing*) The Ides of March are come.

Michael.   (*as Soothsayer*) Ay, Caesar, but not gone.

Piddles.   (*as Cassius*) What, urge you your petitions in the street? Come to the capitol.

SM.   Do I have to?

Michael.   Yes!

SM walks around the stage and ends up where he was when he started. The other actors follow him.

Piddles.   I could be well moved if I were you, but I am constant as the northern star.

Man.   O Caesar.

SM.   Oh, me.

Hatch.   Great Caesar!

SM.   Doth not Brutus bootless kneel?

Agatha.   Speak, hands for me!

SM.   Here it comes.

Montaño.   From the pits of hell, I stab at thee!

Michael.   That's *Moby Dick*.

Montaño.   I know. Whale of a book. (*He laughs. No one joins his laughter.*)

Agatha, the Man, Hatch, Montaño, and Piddles stab SM. Then Michael stabs him.

SM.   Et tu, Brute! Then fall, Caesar!

SM, as Caesar, falls dead.

Man.   Liberty! Freedom! Tyranny is dead!

Piddles.   (*singing*) Do you hear the people sing? ~~Singing the songs of angry men?~~

Michael.   It's not time for a song. And we overkilled *Les Mis* last time.

Piddles.   Sorry.

Man.   Liberty! Freedom! Tyranny is dead!

Michael.   You already said that.

~~Man.   Oh, okay.~~

Montaño.   Your Scottish dialect is gone.

Man.   I was acting.

Agatha.   He's an actor.

Montaño.   I know that.

Michael.   Caesar is dead! I told you he was ambitious!

69

Montaño.   You did. ~~Quite well. We didn't hear it in this script, but you did say it.~~ I read it in high school English.

Match enters and begins a monologue.

Match.   Friends, Romans, countrymen!

Hatch.   Match!! (*Running up to him*)

Match holds up his palm to stop him. Hatch stops.

Match.   (*reverent, sincere*) Friends, Romans, countrymen, lend me your beers.

Michael.   Ears.

Match.   Your ears.

Montaño.   (*laughing*) He said "beers."

Match.   (*Continuing*) I come to bury Caesar, not to praise him. The evil that men do lives after them. The good is oft interred with their bones; So let it be with Caesar.

Hatch claps. Match holds out his hand to stop him.

Match.   The noble Brutus hath told you that Caesar was ambitious.

Michael.   I did.

Piddles.   He did.

Match.   I'll tell you what's ambitious.

Montaño.   Uh-oh. He's going off script.

Match.   Ambition is taking on the responsibility of doing what we're doing on this stage.

Piddles.   What?

Match.   I've had a lot of time to think. ~~And I thought and I've read and I've looked and I've thought.~~ And in looking for myself, I found truth.

Hatch.   You have? I'm proud of you, brother.

Agatha.   You *have* become more talkative.

Match.   I've thought a lot about Beebles.

Michael.   Match . . .

Match.   Wait. I know we were looking and looking, and she came to us. She showed up so we could see her, but I don't know if doing all the shows and searching for why we're doing it and . . . (*gets overwhelmed*)

Michael.   You're experiencing a crisis like I did. ~~I understand, Match.~~ It's normal.

70

Match.   Why do we do this?   We memorize and get on this stage, in this moment.

Piddles, Montaño, and Hatch all stomp a rhythmic stomp.

Piddles.   Sorry. Old habits.

Match.   I worry people won't understand the shows.

SM.   The references.

Match.   Who are you?

SM.   The Stage Manager.

Match.   No, you're not. I just talked with the stage manager.

Michael.   The character of the Stage Manager.

Match.   See? *(frustrated)* Confusion.

Michael.   Not everybody's going to understand everything. That's okay. We keep going, show after show. We do this glorious task. Remember?

Match.   Who are you trying to convince?

Michael.   *(Taken back a bit)* Remember?

Match.   I want to remember. I want to get it.

Montaño.   Maybe we should just *do* it?

Piddles.   What do you mean?

Montaño.   Quit talking. Quit elaborating. Just run these babies. These are all new *references*, right?

Michael.   Right. That's why we're here. I've learned that lesson. We create, but learn from the shows.

SM.   References.

Montaño.   Whatever. Just go. Let's do it. Go!

Piddles.   He's right.

Michael.   *(to Match)* Are you able to do this?

Match.   Maybe.

Michael.   What about handling bigger roles?

Match.   I'll try.

Montaño.   Excellent. Go!

71

Agatha. Wait. Where are Mary Ann and Brannon?

Piddles. (*Obviously trying to avoid the question*) It doesn't matter.

Agatha. ~~What?~~ What do you mean? ~~Where are they?~~

Piddles. People move on. Characters move on. We're written for this moment on this stage.

Man. Who are Mary Ann and Brannon?

Agatha. Characters in "The Beebles Accord"

Piddles. Mary Ann's character is written out. ~~The actress has moved on.~~ (*Beat*) And . . . Brannon . . . (*pauses*) is dead.

Hatch. What?

Agatha. Dead?

Piddles. (*Quickly*) The playwright wrote another short play between these two. He put Brannon in it and killed him off.

~~Match.~~ ~~What?~~

~~Hatch.~~ ~~How awful!~~

~~Agatha.~~ ~~How delicious.~~

Piddles. ~~It was noble. His end was . . . heroic, but Brannon is no more.~~ He was a character.

Hatch. Aren't we all . . . (*realizing his own "character mortality"*) oh.

Montaño. Can we move on? ~~Time's wasting. We're going hyper-speed. With your permission, Michael?~~

~~Michael.~~ ~~Go.~~

~~Piddles.~~ ~~Hyper-speed?~~

~~Michael.~~ ~~Let's try it.~~

Agatha. (*Runs downstage, speaks in a deep British brogue*) And I take the sardine. No, I leave the sardines. No, I take the sardines.

SM. (*Joining her, looking out over the audience to answer her*) You leave the sardines and you hang up the phone.

Michael. Wait. We can't do this play.

Agatha. Yes, right. I hang up the phone.

Michael. Agatha.

72

SM.   And you leave the sardines.

Agatha.   I leave the sardines?

Michael.   Agatha! (*searching for the Stage Manager's name here*) SM!

SM.   SM?

Michael.   I don't know what else to call you. Your character is . . . ?

SM.   (*Certain of the answer, then hesitating, confused.*) Uh. Yeah. Uh.

Michael.   SM.

SM.   Okay.

Agatha.   But I like this play. I want to play Dotty. It's the first role I've felt this connected to since we began.

Michael.   Look around. We don't have the set.

Agatha.   We don't need . . . oh.

SM.   Yeah, the set *is* a major part.

Montaño.   Can we move on?

Michael.   We'll find some way to make "Noises Off" work, just not now. ~~We'll have to build a set.~~

~~Agatha.~~   ~~Is that a promise?~~

~~Michael.~~   ~~It is. Just not now.~~

Match.   Everything is falling apart. I knew it.

~~Piddles.~~   ~~C'mon everybody. Come with me. Let's let Michael and Match tackle this next part.~~

~~Match.~~   ~~No, don't leave. I don't know if I've up for it. I need you guys here.~~

~~Piddles.~~   ~~Okay. We'll sit then.~~

~~*Everyone besides Michael and Match sits on the set.*~~

Michael.   ~~Okay,~~ Match. Think about it. ~~We're staying in Europe. It's~~ the 1890's. ~~High society.~~ The end of the Victorian Age.

~~Man.~~   ~~I know what *this* is.~~

~~Piddles.~~   ~~Shh.~~

~~Michael.~~   ~~Everything is about appearances and status.~~

~~Montaño.~~   ~~It's wild. Get it? (*Giggles*)~~

~~Piddles.   Shh, Montaño.~~

Match.   Michael, I'm not into it.

~~Michael.   Yeah, you are. You can do it. (*acting, British accent*) Besides, your name isn't Jack at all; it's Ernest.~~

~~Match.   Oh.~~

~~Michael.   C'mon. You know the line.~~

~~Match.   I don't remember it.~~

~~Michael.   "It isn't Ernest; it's Jack."~~

~~Match.   Oh, okay. Sorry.~~

~~Michael.   No, that's your line.~~

~~Match.   What is?~~

~~Michael.   "It isn't Earnest; it's Jack."~~

~~Match.   Oh, okay. (*British accent*) It isn't Ernest; it's Jack.~~

~~Michael.   (*Acting*) You have always told me it was Ernest. I have introduced you to every one as Ernest. You answer to the name of Ernest. You look as if your name was Ernest. You are the most earnest-looking person I ever saw in my life. It is perfectly absurd that your name isn't Ernest.~~

~~It's on your cards. Here is one of them. (*He pulls out a card and starts to read.*) Mr. . . .~~

~~Match.   (*grabs the card out of his hand*) No.~~

~~Michael.   You're not supposed to do that. I have to read the card. I don't have that part memorized.~~

~~Match.   No. I can't do this.~~

Piddles.   (*walking up*) Match, what's wrong? Are you okay?

SM.   He said he wasn't into it.

Montaño.   That can't stop us.

Michael.   No, it can't. Not being in the mood to act can never keep an actor from acting. Never. We have a duty. ~~We are in the shows that we . . . are in.~~

~~SM.   And you're not into it, either.~~

~~Michael.   What?~~

~~SM.   I can tell. Your heart isn't in it.~~

74

Michael.	~~Look. You're new here. You don't know me.~~ I admit that I wasn't always where I should be, but I've matured. I know what it means to be a mature actor now.
SM.	Do you?
Montaño.	Watch your attitude, bud!
SM.	Or what? You're going to hit me with another baseball?
Montaño.	Is that a request? I can comply!
Piddles.	Calm down, now. Calm down.
Michael.	(*Frustrated*) I'm faithful. I'm here on this stage, doing what I know we have to do.
Piddles.	We know, Michael. ~~We know.~~
SM.	Do we?
Montaño.	(*to Piddles, looking at SM*) Let me take him out.
Piddles.	No.
Hatch.	No more violence!
Montaño.	There hasn't been any violence. Yet.
SM.	Baseball.
Man.	That *was* pretty cool.
Michael.	Enough! ~~We're not here to play around. We have a task. As Brannon told us last time,~~ the playwright's given us the responsibility to cover the shows, the references. And Match, you can do it, too.
Match.	But some of these, even *I* don't understand.
Michael.	We'll work through it. It's all a mystery, right? ~~There are things that don't make sense.~~
~~Agatha.~~	~~Like a flipped coin?~~
~~Michael.~~	~~What?~~
~~Piddles.~~	~~Always on heads?~~
~~Michael.~~	~~Always on . . . oh! Yeah. (*pretends to flip a coin over and over*) Heads. Heads. Come on!~~
~~Montaño.~~	~~The law of averages, if I have this right, means that if six monkeys were thrown up in the air for long enough they would land on their tails about as often as they would land on their . . .~~

Man.   Heads!

SM.   (*Stepping up on the set*) ~~I will buy with you, sell with you, talk with you, walk with you, and so following, but I will not eat with you, drink with you, nor pray with you. For,~~ if you prick us, do we not bleed? If you tickle us, do we not laugh? If you poison us, do we not die? And if you wrong us, shall we not revenge?

Piddles.   Very nice. ~~Very nice.~~

Michael.   Not bad.

Montaño.   I'd like to see him try Shylock, though.

Hatch.   That was Shylock.

Montaño.   I mean Shylock from "The Merchant of Venice."

Hatch.   That *was* Shylock.

Agatha.   From "The Merchant of Venice."

Montaño.   Well, it didn't sound like it. I would have chosen the part about ~~a horse, of course, of course.~~

Piddles.   ~~What?~~

Montaño.   ~~In "The Merchant of Venice" when Skylock is in desperation. He says, "Every tale condemns me for a villain."~~ A horse of course, of course, my kingdom, of course.

Michael.   Montaño, that's "Richard III."

Montaño.   I don't care if he said it three or even four times.

Michael.   No, the play, "Richard III." And it's "a horse, a horse, my kingdom for a horse."

Montaño.   ~~I get something a little mixed up, and everybody goes nuts.~~

Michael.   ~~It's okay. We're just getting it all straight.~~

Match.   ~~(*affecting a hunched back*) Now is the winter of our discontent, made glorious summer by this sun of York.~~

Hatch.   ~~Match, that's great.~~

Match.   ~~I actually know that one. I played Richard years ago.~~

Piddles.   ~~Really?~~

Match.   ~~Believe it or not, I did.~~

Man.   ~~(*to Michael*) Can he *do* that?~~

Michael.   ~~What?~~

76

Man. Play Richard with the *back problem*, you know.

Michael. As a hunchback?

Man. Shhh! Can you say that?

Michael. For *now*. That's Richard III. It's a part of Shakespeare's character. It's an integral part of the script.

Hatch. (*to Match*) You'd better drop the back thing now. It could be offensive.

Match. It's fun.

Hatch. Not if it were real.

Match straightens up.

Montaño. You all know what's next!

Agatha. I forgot.

SM. Me, too. What's he talking about.

Montaño. All *hell's* gonna break loose!

Piddles. Language! You can't say that.

Montaño. If it's literal, yes, I can. You know what's coming!

Agatha. Oh!

Montaño. Get ready to bust up through the floor. We're going back to the 1500's again!

Michael. Okay, Montaño. Get ready.

Montaño. Oh, I'm ready.

Michael. (*while everyone is scrambling to get low on the floor at various places*) Match, remember that you're coming collect him.

Match. Wait. What? Me? Oh, those are my lines?

Montaño. Match, you know these!

Match. No, wait. I don't. I knew Richard, but I don't know these.

Michael. You've got it. They'll come to you. Go, Montaño.

Montaño. Was this the face that launch'd a thousand ships. And burnt the topless towers of Ilium? Sweet Helen, make me immortal with a kiss. (*laughs*)

Michael. (*to Match*) That's your line.

Match. I don't know it.

Michael. ~~Yes, you do.~~

Match. ~~No, I don't.~~

Montaño. ~~(*repeating himself*) Sweet Helen, make me immortal with a kiss. *(laughs)*~~

Michael. ~~Match!~~

Law enters with stealth and power ~~and takes over Match's part.~~

Law. ~~Thus to we ascend to view those souls which sin seals the black souls of hell. And, this gloomy night, here in his room, will wretched Faustus be.~~

Montaño. ~~What shall become of Faustus, being in hell forever? God forbade it, indeed; but Faustus hath done it: for the vain pleasure of four and twenty years hath Faustus lost eternal joy and felicity. I writ them a bill with mine own blood: the date is expired; this is the time, and he will fetch me.~~

Law. ~~What, weep'st thou?~~ 'tis too late; ~~despair! Farewell.~~ Fools that will laugh on earth must weep in hell.

Montaño. Impose some end to my incessant pain; Let Faustus ~~live in hell a thousand years, A hundred thousand, and at last be sav'd! No end is limited to damned souls.~~

The other actors as devils come and start to pull Montaño down below the set—or upstage.

Montaño. ~~I'll burn my book! Ahhh!!~~

The all come up for air. They congratulate Montaño and hug Law.

Piddles. Law!

Michael. Law, how are you?

Hatch. I didn't expect to see you.

Agatha. How did I know you couldn't stay away?

Law. Well, you needed a devil, and what better character than a lawyer?

Match. Good point.

Man. Who is this?

Piddles. This is Law, our friend from the first . . . show about Beebles.

Law. ~~Where is Beebles?~~

Hatch. ~~She's with Colton.~~

Law. ~~I heard about the Swedish supermodel.~~

Piddles. ~~What?~~

Agatha. ~~She was Swedish?~~

Michael. ~~Let's change the subject.~~

Piddles. ~~A few of us heard Beebles earlier.~~

Michael. ~~It wasn't Beebles.~~

SM. ~~It was definitely a cow's bellow.~~

Michael. ~~It wasn't. It could have been anything.~~

Hatch. ~~It was a bellow.~~

Michael. ~~Law, it's best to drop it.~~

Law. You know, a lot has happened since the last Beebles' show.

Michael. Well, technically, when the lights went out, the show ended, and nothing in this reality has happened again until this one, the "Beebles Refrain" began.

Law. So, that's what he called it? "The Beebles Refrain." Clever. Good. But there were events between the two shows. ~~I see that you've become a leader, Michael.~~

Michael. ~~I'm trying.~~

~~Hatch. We lost a few people.~~

~~Law. I heard.~~

Piddles. You know about it?

Law. I was in the show with Brannon. ~~It was a short ten-minute play, but~~ I was there.

Piddles. I didn't know.

Law. It's okay. ~~It was a special time, and~~ because of it, I've been searching for myself.

SM. Just what we need: another one of you going all emotionally unstable.

Law. Who's this?

Montaño. Nobody.

SM. I'm The Stage Manager.

Michael. From the first show we referenced.

Law. Ah. "Our Town"?

Michael. Yeah.

Law. Okay. (*ignoring SM*) For the record, I'm not emotionally unstable. I'm just coming to grips with the nature of being a character. Michael, I understand what

79

you were dealing with: learning to play our parts ~~and the like. I'm not rebelling. I'm just wondering my role in all of this.~~

Piddles.   You're Law. You stand for what is right and just.

Law.   I hope. But I'm seriously considering changing my name.

Agatha.   Can you do that?

Hatch.   Can *we* do that?

Law.   I don't know. I'll have to ~~go through the legal channels and~~ find out, maybe contact the playwright himself. I just don't know if Law encompasses who I am anymore.

Montaño.   What are you thinking?

Law.   Instead of Law, maybe "Justice"

Michael.   Uh, okay.

Law.   I don't know. I may go through a transition period. Maybe you guys could get used to calling me "The Character Formally Known as Law"?

Montaño.   That whole thing? As your name?

Law.   Maybe?

Match.   That's princely.

Piddles.   Until you figure it out, can we just call you Law? We don't have much time. This is a one-act.

Law.   (*Sighs*) For now.

SM.   I knew actors were crazy, but are characters becoming emotionally unstable as well? We have a reluctant leader, an overemotional twin, and a lawyer with an identity crisis.

Man.   You know, you deserved that baseball.

Law.   As a character, I did come right from that short play to this very scene. I'm still reeling a bit from the sting. Just give me a few minutes.

Agatha.   Actors can be a bit emotional and sometimes irrational. Perhaps that's what makes them able to represent characters that face the same variety of strengths and weaknesses of being human. The instability of the characters themselves could very well be a symbol for the role actors play in giving themselves so completely to becoming the characters. Of course, I'm trying to understand the playwright, as a writer myself, you know.

SM.   Or serve as a mouthpiece for him.

80

Hatch. ~~(*Starts crying*) Ohhh.~~

Match. ~~(*Deep breath*) It's okay, Hatch. I'm right here.~~

Hatch. ~~It's not that. I was just thinking about what Agatha said.~~

Match. ~~She said a lot. As usual.~~

Hatch. ~~About actors taking on the weaknesses and flaws of the characters.~~

Agatha. ~~Are you upset as the actor or the character?~~

Hatch. ~~I'm not upset for me.~~

Match. ~~What's the deal, then?~~

Hatch. ~~Just thinking about Heath Ledger.~~

Michael. ~~Whoa! No names.~~

Montaño. ~~Why so serious?~~

Piddles. ~~Montaño , let's not.~~

Man.   I like this troupe.

SM.   I don't.

Montaño.   That's because you're an . . . (*looks out over the audience, hesitates, wants to say it but edits himself*) you're an . . . you're a . . . donkey.

SM.   Your sticks and stones are weak.

Montaño lunges toward SM, but Michael and Match stop him.

Montaño.   I'll cram sticks and stones where the sun don't shine.

Michael.   (*Loudly*) We have a task! We are characters given a duty! And we WILL perform that duty. (*to SM*) Stop being antagonistic!

SM.   Me?

Michael.   Yes, you. We all get along. You're the poison in the soup.

SM.   Perhaps that's because I'm the only one here focused enough to . . .

Michael.   Enough! You're crossing a line. I've seen actors replaced for years. Characters are a different story.

SM.   What are you saying?

Montaño.   (*Sneering*) You know what happens to problematic characters.

SM.   I'm a creation of this playwright just like you are.

81

Michael.   (*Making the point that SM had better be careful*) Exactly.

Agatha.   (*Reiterating Michael's point*) Exactly.

Piddles.   (*Reiterating Michael's point*) Exactly.

SM.   This isn't fair. You've been in the Beebles' universe longer.

Man.   *I* haven't.

SM.   (*Frustrated.*) I'm the way I was made. This is who I am.

Montaño.   Look who's emotional now!

SM.   This is who I was *written* to be.

Match.   Here we go again.

Piddles.   Michael, we have work to do.

Michael.   You're right. Go!

Piddles.   Half circle. Greek chorus.

Everyone scrambles to create a half circle with Piddles in the focus of the parabola.

SM is slow-to-move.

Montaño.   She said move!

SM moves into place.

Piddles.   Stronger than lover's love is lover's hate. Incurable, in each, the wounds they make. (*pause*) Hate is a bottomless cup; I will pour and pour.

Law.   Wait. Is this . . . ?

Piddles.   I know indeed what evil I intend to do, but stronger than all my afterthoughts is my fury, fury that brings upon mortals the greatest evils.

Law.   Wait. There's no law or justice in this play.

Michael.   ~~It's a play, for goodness sake. Go with it.~~

Piddles.   ~~I understand too well the dreadful act I'm going to commit, but my judgement can't check my anger, and that incites the greatest evils human beings do.~~

Montaño.   Piddles, I'm sorry. I can't do this.

Law.   I can't either.

Michael.   What are you doing?

Montaño.   I'm sorry. I hate this play. "Medea" freaks me out! ~~It's so cold, so cruel. I'm talking her and Jason both. I just can't.~~

Agatha. ~~It's so perfect. You're an idealist.~~

SM. ~~I don't suppose I'm allowed an opinion.~~

Michael. (*ignoring him*) I'm so sorry, Piddles. ~~This isn't fair to you. This role . . .~~

Piddles. I hate it.

Michael. What?

Piddles. I hate it. I never wanted to play Medea. I'm more of a Brechtian, Williamsy, Becket-like, Shawite modern woman.

Michael. (*looks at her with admiration*) You know your stuff.

Piddles. I do. In fact . . .

She rushes whisper in Montaño 's ear. He smiles and nods.

Montaño. Sure!

Michael. What?

Piddles. You'll see. Hide behind the set. All of you, except Montaño.

They cautiously move behind the set. SM is the slowest.

Piddles. Move it, SM.

Montaño. (*in an Irish dialect*) When I cast my mind back to that summer of 1936, different kinds of memories offer themselves to me. We got our first wireless set that summer. ~~Well, a sort of a set, and it obsessed us. It arrived as August was about too begin.~~ In the old days August the first was La Lughnasa, and the days ~~and weeks of harvesting~~ that followed were called the Festival of Lughnasa.

Match. Are we cross-gender acting?

Piddles. Yes!

Match, Hatch, Piddles, and Michael enter as sisters and begin to pantomime the opening actions of "Dancing at Lughnasa" they busy themselves with their tasks. PIDDLES (as MAGGIE) makes a mash for hens. MATCH (as AGNES) knits gloves. HATCH (as ROSE) carries a basket of turf into the kitchen and empties it into the large box beside the range. MICHAEL (as CHRIS) irons at the kitchen table. They all work in silence. Then CHRIS stops ironing, goes to the tiny mirror on the wall and scrutinizes her face.

Michael. When are we going to get a decent mirror to see ourselves in?

Piddles. You can see enough to do you.

Michael. I'm going to throw this aul cracked thing out.

83

Piddles.   Indeed you're not, Chrissie. I'm the one that broke it and the only way to avoid seven years bad luck is to keep on using it.

Michael.   You can see nothing in it.

Match.   Except more and more wrinkles.

Michael.   D'you know what I think I might do? I think I just might start wearing lipstick.

Match.   ~~Do you hear this, Maggie?~~

Piddles.   ~~Steady on, girl. Today it's lipstick; tomorrow it's the gin bottle.~~

~~*Work continues. Nobody speaks. Then suddenly and unexpectedly Hatch bursts into raucous song.*~~

Hatch.   ~~'Will you come to Abyssinia, will you come? Bring your own cup and saucer and a bun...'~~

~~*As he sings the next two lines he* dances *— a gauche, graceless shuffle that defies the rhythm of the song.*~~

Hatch.   ~~'Mussolini will be there with his airplanes in the air, Will you come to Abyssinia, will you come? ——— Not bad, Maggie — eh?~~

Piddles tries to light a very short cigarette butt.

Piddles.   ~~You should be on the stage,~~ Rose.

Law (as Kate) enters. Everyone gets quiet.

Law.   Why do all of you look so happy? This is supposed to be an Irish family in an Irish play!

Radio music begins playing.

Law.   What's that ungodly noise?

Michael.   It's called music, Kate. Instruments. Chords.

Michael, Piddles, Match, and Hatch all shake and quiver from wanting to dance, but show self restraint as they look at Law.

Finally, Match, as Agnes, speaks with intensity.

Match.   How many years has it been since we were at the harvest dance? - at any dance? ~~And I don't care how young they are, how drunk and dirty and sweaty they are.~~ I want to dance, Kate. It's the festival of Lughnasa. I'm only thirty-five. I want to dance.

Michael, Piddles, Match, and Hatch break out into crazy dance. Law looks at them,

controlling his anger.

Law taps his foot, looks down at it, and purposefully stops it from tapping.

Agatha goes to Law.

Agatha.   (*Loudly, over the music*) Isn't this the part in Lughnasa where Kate gives in and dances with her sisters? Isn't that what you're supposed to do?

The music abruptly stops as Michael, Piddles, Match, and Hatch stop dancing at stare at Agatha. She has ruined the scene and the momentum of what was about to happen. Law, oblivious, flings his head back, in the silence, and omits a loud "Yaaah" as he begins to dance, very badly. Everyone stares at him. After six or seven seconds, he stops, out of breath and stares at everyone.

Law.   What?

Piddles.   Agatha ruined the moment.

Agatha.   Me?

Piddles.   Yes. He was about to join us.

Agatha.   But . . .

Piddles.   But you blared it out to the audience.

Hatch.   ~~(*to Law*) Your dancing was really bad anyway.~~

Law.   ~~I never claimed to be a dancer. I'm an officer of the . . . law.~~

SM.   ~~Well, that was a failure.~~

Michael.   ~~That's enough.~~

Man.   ~~You guys are better that I thought. That was a good scene.~~

Piddles.   ~~Until it was ruined. (*looks at Agatha*)~~

Agatha.   ~~It's my job to state the obvious. It's like . . . foreshadowing.~~

Piddles.   ~~There's a difference between foreshadowing and trolling.~~

Agatha.   ~~Trolling? We're not online.~~

Piddles.   ~~But we're onstage.~~

SM.   This is insane. How did I get written into this disaster?

Montaño.   (*upset with SM*) Michael!

Michael.   Just act!

Montaño begins to run around wailing ~~as if he's the early version of Helen Keller from "The Miracle Worker." The other characters step back. Eventually Piddles goes up to Montaño and~~

85

calms him. She begins forming sign letters with her fingers and putting them into his hand. He seems to understand for a second, then runs off wild again.

Michael.　　　*(As Captain Arthur Keller)* Young lady! You must convince me that there's the slightest hope of you teaching a child who now flees from you like the plague.

Piddles.　　　*(as Annie Sullivan)* There isn't. It's hopeless here.

SM.　　　Hopeless. *(The other actors glare at him.)*

Michael.　　　Am I to understand . . .

Piddles.　　　We all agree it's hopeless here. The next question is . . .

SM.　　　Why are you doing this?

Match, very upset, goes to sit far downstage.

Hatch follows him to comfort him.

Michael.　　　*(to SM)* I think it's time that you go.

SM.　　　Just disappear.

Law.　　　Your presence *is* rather damaging.

Piddles.　　　Why is it that there is always, *always* one character or one actor that can ruin everything for the rest of the group? It never fails.

SM.　　　Well, I can't just leave. ~~I'm here.~~ You should know how things work.

Man.　　　Oeeeeeeeeeedipus!!

Michael.　　　What?

Man.　　　Oeeeeeeeeeedipus!!

Piddles.　　　Really?

Law.　　　Wait.

Agatha.　　　Are we doing this again?

Hatch.　　　Doing what? I'm confused.

Match.　　　See!

Piddles.　　　Going off-script again. Oedipus is not in this script. I don't like Greek tragedies. I would have remembered.

Michael.　　　Is there some reason . . . ?

Montaño.　　　(entering) Greetings! Or should I say WOE!?!

Piddles.　　　Montaño, what are you doing?

Montaño.   I'm not Montaño. I'm the Oracle of Delphi.

Michael.   Montaño, this is not . . .

Montaño.   Trust me. Okay?

Michael.   (sighs) Okay.

Montaño.   I am the Oracle of Delphi.   And this (*motions off-stage*) is . . . (*a man in a mask enters*) Oedipus.

Piddles.   Who's that?

Faux Oedipus (FO).   I'm Oedipus.

Hatch.   No, really? Who are you?

Montaño.   He is Oedipus. And I have a prophecy for him!

Match.   Great.

Montaño.   And you (*points to SM*) are Laius, the father of Oedipus.

SM.   Wait a minute here.

Montaño.   And you (*to Piddles*) are Jocasta, the mother of Oedipus.

Piddles.   Ewwww.

SM.   I'm not doing this anymore. (*Moves to the top of the set and crosses his arms.*)

Piddles.   ~~I don't know any of these lines.~~

Montaño.   ~~You don't need to. Oedipus. Echo me on that part, Man.~~

Man.   ~~Okay.~~

Montaño.   Oedipus!

Man.   ~~Oeeeeeeeeeeeedipus!~~

Montaño.   Know this, your fate. You shall kill your father and marry your mother.

Piddles.   This is why I hate Greek plays.

SM.   Wait a minute.

FO.   No! I shall not allow this fate.

Michael.   I know that voice.

FO.   I shall cross the entirety of Greece to run from this prophecy.

FO runs in circles and ends up at the set.

FO.   Move, old man. You are in my way.

87

SM.   I'm not playing this game.

FO.   I said move from this narrow path on the edge of this high mountain so that I can continue. I shall say please just once.

SM.   I'm not doing this.

FO.   You won't move.

SM.   No, I won't act anymore. I'm not playing Laius.

FO.   Then I shall come by you anyway.

SM.   Don't come up here.

FO goes to the top of the set and starts to shove SM.

SM.   Stop. I'm not doing this.

FO.   I'm just trying to get past you, old man.

SM.   Stop. Seriously. Stop.

FO bumps into SM and causes him to fall off the set. He lies lifeless.

Piddles.   Wait. What just happened?

FO turns and faces the audience. His arms are crossed.

Michael.   Hey. (*walking toward SM*) Hey!

Montaño.   He can't hear you.

Hatch.   What?

Match.   (*Getting up*) What?

Agatha.   (*Excited*) Is this what I think this is?

Michael.   He can't. He's "The Stage Manager."

Montaño.   Well . . .

Michael.   (*to Faux Oedipus*) And who are you? You just . . .   You didn't . . .

The Grim Reaper enters.

Grim.   Am I in the right place?

Montaño.   Yes. I heard you were coming!

Piddles.   What's going on? Are you . . . ?

Grim.   ~~Probably.~~ The outfit gives it away, right?

Michael.   Are you saying that SM . . . ? And you're the . . . ?

88

Grim.   Well, I started out a long, long time ago. ~~I don't really remember when.~~ I've
            been doing my business for a few millennia. ~~A few hundred years back, a couple
            of brothers tried to steal my name, starting telling tales of my business and all. I
            took care of them, and I take care of people now.~~ I must say that it's been a while
            since I've been on a real stage. ~~I did a bit of acting back in high school, but that
            was long before plays were a thing. But to be called on a stage to get a real
            character is a treat.~~

Michael.   He's dead. Not pretend dead? Not fake dead? Dead.

Montaño.   Dead.

Michael.   (*to Montaño*) What'd you do?

Montaño.   Not much. I was, you know, ~~Helen Keller, all, uggh and waah and blah-do-blah~~
            and there was Faux Oedipus standing there in his mask. I was all, "Whoa. Wait a
            minute. This isn't part of the show." Then he told me who was and that—are you
            ready for this—the playwright sent him to come and get rid SM, in character, in
            scene.

Michael.   What?

Montaño.   The guy wasn't doing his job. He was counterproductive. You know it.

~~Hatch.   That's true.~~

~~Agatha.   That is true.~~

Montaño.   His character didn't fit in with the rest of the show. And since he is a character,
            you know, . . .

Piddles.   The playwright wrote him out.

Montaño.   Exactly.

Law.   Whoa.

Michael.   (*to Faux Oedipus*) But who are you?

Montaño.   He was brought back to help us out.

Piddles.   Brought back?

FO removes his mask to reveal Brannon from the previous Beebles play.

Everyone.   Brannon!!

Everyone except Michael and Montaño gathers around Brannon to hug him.

Michael.   Brought him back?

Montaño.   Well, the playwright can do whatever he wants, right?

FO.   Hello, everyone. Careful. Careful. Newly alive here.

Piddles.   You're alive!

FO.   Yes, I seem to be. I have a tendency to die quite a bit.   This time the resurrection
           was a bit abrupt.

Hatch.   It's so good to see you, sir!

Man.   This is the famous Brannon?

FO.   And this is?

Hatch.   This is the man.

FO.   The man?

Piddles.   A character in this show

FO.   If I may ask a favor, could you all refrain from calling me Brannon? That name
           has a deathly stigma for me. Please call me FO from now own, for Faux Oedipus.
           It's not the most pleasant name in the world, but neither is Brannon anymore, and
           well, we're on the stage. FO for Faux Oedipus.

Michael.   Really?

FO.   Really.

Piddles.   We can do that. (*She hugs him.*)

FO.   Please. Please. Okay. Thanks.

Grim.   Can I please do my job?

Piddles.   Of course, I guess.

Grim.   I mean, I'm trying here. It's not a fun task. Seriously. And this stage thing
           freaks me out a bit. The last time I was on stage, it was supposedly in Swindon,
           England, but I doubt I was really there. And they told me it was 1998, but it
           couldn't be. I guess it could be 1998 during the actual play. I just show up where
           you all need me. It was for some dog named Wellington that had been stabbed
           with some sort of garden utensil. A kid named Christopher, excuse me, (*British
           accent*) *ChristahFUH*, was freaking out and wailing. Well, I guess he was a kid.
           He was, according to him, 15 years, 3 months, and 2 days old. It was odd. And
           it was on stage, which caught me off guard.

Montaño.   What a curious incident

Hatch.   And it was about a dog?

Match.   In the night-time?

90

Michael.   (*to Grim*) Are you who you say you are?

Grim.   Unfortunately. (*Beat*) And there's a dead body over there.

Michael.   Can "The Stage Manager" actually die?

Law.   If it's written in the script

Michael.   ~~Well, yeah. I guess.~~

Grim.   ~~You may not like it, but I'm here.~~

Hatch.   ~~And we're down an actor.~~

Agatha.   ~~We are. But we've covered quite a few plays.~~

FO.   ~~——~~You've referenced several shows already then?

Michael.   ~~We have.~~

FO.   ~~I respect that.~~ Could you use some help in doing some more?

Piddles.   Would you?

FO.   Sure. Why not? I'm here.

Grim.   Is no one going to ask me?

Michael.   ~~What?~~

Grim.   ~~I'm on stage.~~ That dead guy's not going anywhere.

Michael.   (*looking out over the audience*) Our playwright's a strange man, strange.

Montaño.   But he fixed our problem.

Match.   By killing someone!

Hatch.   A character.

Piddles.   (to Grim) You want to act?

Grim.   ~~I'm well-known for my job, but~~ as an actor, I'm pretty much a dark horse.

Montaño.   (*Excited, stepping forward*) A dark horse?

Piddles.   What?

Montaño.   A horse?! Horses? They saw me. They saw what I did. They saw my sin.

Michael.   Montaño

Montaño.   A young man. Horses. A crime. Must find the reason.

Montaño starts pulling off some clothes. He pulls off his shirt, runs to the top of the set and pulls off his shoes and socks. Before he stops, he has unbuttoned his pants, but he has NOT pulled them down.

During this whole time, Michael, Law, FO, and Piddles are screaming for him to stop.

Piddles.   Montaño!

Michael.   No, Montaño. You can't do that!

Law.   We can't do "Equus" on this stage!

FO.   Montaño , keep your clothes on! For goodness sake!

Montaño stops.

Montaño.   All you ever do is stop me.

Match.   All you ever do is strip.

Montaño.   "Equus" is a Tony-Award-winning play

Michael.   That we can't do in this show

Match.   You're pretty bad about going to extremes.

FO.   Please put your shirt back on.

Montaño puts his shirt back on, but does not put his socks and shoes back on.

Montaño.   You're no fun.

Agatha.   I thought it was fun.

Grim.   You ought to see some of the things I've seen. Nothing would shock you. ~~People are crazy. I mean crazy.~~

FO.   Michael, this is "The Beebles Refrain," right?

Michael.   ~~I think so. Yes.~~ Unless I've lost my mind, yes.

FO.   And that means . . . ?

Michael.   We are here, ~~all of us,~~ as a result of our original connection with Beebles.

~~Man.~~   ~~Except for me.~~

~~Piddles.~~   ~~But you're one of us now.~~

~~Hatch.~~   ~~Yeah, you are.~~

~~Man.~~   ~~I am?~~

~~Piddles.~~   ~~Of course.~~

Michael.   And when we're on this stage, we are living out the vision of what we learned during our unity, our accord. We are characters playing characters. Actors are our characters playing our characters for the sake of characters.

Match.   My head hurts.

FO.   And, Michael, you've got it. ~~Yes, sir!~~

Michael.   We don't age. We stay who we are.

FO.   Because on this stage, time is not an issue.

Michael.   No matter how many times we perform this play, our characters will . . .

Piddles.   Still be the same. Oh!

Montaño.   Wait. That's the testament about time. That art is the enemy . . .

Michael.   Of TIME.

Hatch.   Oh.

Man.   This whole experience is pretty awesome. On this stage.

Piddles.   On this stage, you guys.

Everyone.   On this stage. (*Left foot stomp, right foot stomp twice, left foot stomp*)

Piddles.   That's what I'm talking about.

Match.   Wait a minute. We are eternal?

Law.   As characters. Yes. Forever in the script. Forever in the memory.

Match.   Oh, it's starting to make sense.

Michael.   And we do have the power of creation, to make ~~new things and~~ new experiences. ~~We also bring what we have to that which is already engraved into the art of humanity.~~

~~FO.~~   ~~That's what I've figured out. And it took dying a few times for me to get it. You're ahead of the game.~~

Michael.   And we are as strong as our lines

~~FO.~~   ~~And our ability to deliver them well.~~

~~Michael.~~   ~~So, Aunt Martha, Aunt Abby, how did he die?~~

~~Agatha and Piddles run up to assume the roles of Aunt Martha and Aunt Abby.~~

~~Agatha.~~   ~~Oh, Mortimer, don't be so inquisitive. The gentleman died because he drank some wine with poison in it.~~

Michael.   Well, how did the poison get in the wine?

Piddles.   Well, we put in wine because it's less noticeable. When it's in tea it has a distinct odor.

Law.   Bravo!

Hatch.   I love that play!

Michael.   Take this. (*Throws him a long, fake nose.*) You know what to do.

Hatch.   Seriously?

Michael.   Go for it.

Hatch.   (*as Cyrano*) A great nose may be an index of a great soul!

Match.   Oh, my friend, can you help me win the love of Roxanne?

Montaño.   (*starts singing "Roxanne" from the Police/"Moulin Rouge"*) ROXANNE!

Michael.   No. Not here. This is the original.

Montaño.   Cyrano! Are you okay?

Hatch.   I'm not well.

Match.   Looking for love in all the wrong places.

Michael.   You stop, too.

Hatch.   A lifetime later, and I still was unable to tell the woman I love that I love her.

Hatch gets weaker and weaker and starts to die.

Agatha.   (*as Roxanne*) All those letters, they were you. All those beautiful powerful words, they were you! The voice from the shadows, that was you. You always loved me!

Piddles.   (*singing*) And I-I-I will always love you, I-I will always love you!

Michael.   Piddles!

Law.   Copyright!

Agatha.   Live, for I love you!

Hatch.   No, In fairy tales when to the ill-starred prince the lady says 'I love you,' all his ugliness fades fast—but I remain the same, up to the last!

Agatha.   I have marred your life. I, I . . .

Hatch.   You blessed my life! Never on me had rested woman's love. My mother even could not find me fair: I had no sister; and, when grown a man, I feared the

94

mistress who would mock at me. But I have had your friendship—grace to you. A woman's charm has passed across my path.

Hatch dies.

Agatha cries.

Piddles, Match, Man, Grim, and Law clap.

Piddles.   That was beautiful, just beautiful.

FO.   Well done.

Piddles.   Are you alive?

Hatch.   Yeah, I'm here.

Grim.   Good. I don't like two at once. Messy. And it's a muscle strain.

Michael.   (*tossing Grim a set of keys*) Here. Give it a shot.

Grim.   Me? Really?

Michael.   Yeah, you. He wrote you in this play for some reason.

Grim.   But you know what my field of expertise is.

Michael.   Why do you think I tossed you the keys?

Grim.   (*realizing what they mean*) Oooh!

Michael.   Yeah.

Piddles.   (to Michael) His field of expertise is . . . death.

Michael.   Exactly.

Grim.   I tell you, boys, and you listen to me, boys. Learn this lesson. Be liked and you will never want. You take me, for instance. I never have to wait in line to see a buyer. 'Willy Loman is here!' That's all they have to know, and I go right through." That's the life of a salesman, I tell you. And one of the greatest men I ever knew, he died the death of a salesman, in his green velvet slippers in the smoker of the New York, New Haven, and Hartford, going into Boston—when he died, hundreds of salesmen and buyers were at the funeral. That's a successful life. That's a beloved man.

Montaño.   (*Signing to the tune of "Honesty"*) Irony is just such a lonely word.

Match.   That's impressive.

Montaño.   Thank you.

Match.   I was talking to Grim.

95

Agatha. ~~Burn!~~

Law. ~~And then BOOM.~~

Agatha. ~~What?~~

Law. ~~And then BOOM. In the play. Not your "burn." After Willy Loman's speeches, he takes his keys and then BOOM.~~

Grim. ~~And then I'd be called. To the stage. Again.~~

FO. ~~Called to the stage.~~

Michael. ~~You caught that, too?~~

Piddles. ~~(looking around) Called to the stage.~~

Match. But what if it doesn't turn out right? Or if we're not as perfect as we need to be?

Hatch. It doesn't matter.

Law. It doesn't matter.

Man. The show must go on.

Agatha. The show must go on.

Michael. The show must go on.

Piddles. (*Quoting Queen's song,* ~~with the song's rhythm~~) Inside my ~~heart is breaking, my make-up may be flaking, but my smile still stays on.~~

Montaño. Go on!

Michael. Two households, both alike in dignity,

In fair Verona, where we lay our scene,

From ancient grudge break to new mutiny,

Where civil blood makes civil hands unclean.

Man. ~~Oh! I know this one.~~

Montaño runs up to and climbs the ladder.

Montaño. Romeo!

Piddles. Wait!

Montaño. What?

Piddles. Are you playing Juliet?

Montaño. Sure. Why not?

Piddles.   Because . . . what do I play? Romeo.

Montaño.   Sure. Why not? Be the Romeo you want to see in the world!

~~Law.   Do you bite you tongue at us, sir?~~

~~Michael.   Good. Keep it going.~~

Piddles.   But, soft, what light through yonder window breaks?

            It is the east, and Juliet is the sun.

Match.   That which we call a rose

            By any other name would smell as sweet.

Montaño.   Aren't I Juliet? What are you doing?

Match.   Being the Juliet I want to see in the world.

FO.   A plague o' both your houses!

Michael.   Romeo, Romeo, Romeo! Here's drink: I drink to thee.

~~Agatha.   Parting is such sweet sorrow.~~

Montaño.   (*Quickly and dramatically*) O happy dagger,

            This is thy sheath: there rust, and let me die.

~~Hatch.   All are punished.~~

Michael.   For never was a story of more woe

            Than this of Juliet and her Romeo.

Piddles.   Bravo!

~~Law.   I didn't realize that was actually in the script. It just flowed, though.~~

Montaño.   It's the transition to . . .

The lights flash and loud Polka music begins.

Michael.   (*yelling*) No. Wrong music.

The music stops.

Montaño.   It's the transition to . . .

The lights flash and loud hip-hop music begins.

Michael.   (*yelling*) No! No! That was the wrong music, too.

FO.   Track 14.

The lights flash and ominous, spooky music begins. The characters move to create a large, varied tableau across the stage.

Michael.   There you go. And here we go.

FO.   I am thy father's spirit,

             Doom'd for a certain term to walk the night.

             ~~Revenge his foul and most unnatural murther.~~

Hatch.   Neither a borrower nor a lender be;
             ~~For loan oft loses both itself and friend,~~
             ~~and borrowing dulls the edge of husbandry.~~

Agatha.   This above all: to thine own self be true

Man.   And it must follow, as the night the day,
             thou canst not then be false to any man.

Match.   Wait. Be true?

Michael.   We're in Hamlet, Match.

Match.   I know that, but . . .

Montaño.   Doubt that the sun doth move, doubt truth to be a liar, but never doubt I love.

Match.   Doubt? Doubt that we love?

Piddles.   Are you all right, Match?

Match.   We've lost track of Beebles.

Law.   A little more than kin, and less than kind

Piddles.   She's with Colton. She's not here anymore.   I understand that.

Agatha.   This is the very ecstasy of love.

Match.   But it's more than that. Beebles is what we look for, what we strive for.

Grim.   Though this be madness, yet there is method in 't.

Piddles.   ~~Oh, Match. I know. I know.~~ We know Beebles. She was such a part of making
             us good. ~~She kept us going.~~

Man.   The lady doth protest too much, methinks.

Michael.   Match, you're having misgivings. You're still struggling. I understand.

FO.   When sorrows come, they come not single spies, but in battalions.

Match. Beebles is important, but she's even more important because she helped us realize why we do what we do.

Piddles. Because we could look at her and see goodness~~. . . and innocence~~

Montaño. To be, or not to be: that is the question. Whether 'tis nobler in the mind to suffer the slings and arrows of outrageous fortune . . .

Michael. ~~And~~ she helped us to see what we could be if we stopped focusing on ourselves.

Montaño. . . . and by opposing, end them.

Michael. We're characters and we're here a short time.

Man. The play 's the thing wherein I'll catch the conscience of the king.

Michael. The play's the thing.

Piddles. The play's the thing.

Match. The play's the thing.

FO. This play.

Hatch. This play?

FO. This play. You're characters. One and all. What is your role? And what is your responsibility.

Agatha. To the script

Man. And to the play

Michael. To be faithful while we're here

FO. So, Grim. What's your decision?

Piddles. What decision?

Grim. Obviously, this one. (He moves his arm toward SM)

SM. (Standing up) What a piece of work is man! How noble in reason! How infinite in faculty! In form and moving how express and admirable! ~~in action how like an angel! In apprehension how like a god! The beauty of the world, the paragon of animals!~~

Montaño. What?

Agatha. SM?

Man. How?

Michael. He was . . . (looks at FO, then at SM) Wait. Who are you?

99

Piddles.	Was he dead?
FO.	Oh, yes. Very dead.
SM.	But I'm here. ~~Very much here.~~
Hatch.	But, Michael, you said "The Stage Manager" couldn't die, ~~but then he did, but now he's not. I'm confused.~~
~~Match.~~	~~Wait a minute.~~
~~Agatha.~~	~~This is a reverse of what I normally deal with.~~
Michael.	If he was written as dead, how could you just bring him back?
Piddles.	You brought him back?
Grim.	~~Well, this show is a comedy, ultimately.~~ You just can't have people arbitrarily dying, ~~you know, with all the sorrow and unresolved pain.~~
FO.	And a wise decision it was.
SM.	And I thank you. I have a bit more clarity of thought now.
FO.	(to SM) Isn't that the truth? The third time's the charm, though.
Michael.	I'm trying to make sense of this.
Match.	(to Grim) Are you? And that makes us . . . ?
Grim.	(*Walking around, looking at everyone*) You are so special. You get to live forever. You get to live forever. Look around you. This stage, these lights, this floor, this experience. ~~If the paper you're written on it burned, if the files containing your lines are lost or erased, if the video recording, legal or illegal, is destroyed, you are still immortal because you lived and walked on this stage.~~ Humans live, age, and die, but the essence of who they are lives on because you live. You are here now. Soon, this performance will be memory, but it's forever etched in time. Humanity preserves the best and strongest of what we are in art. Here. On this stage, ~~in a song, on a canvas, in a block of marble, and in the memory of those who are open to it.~~
~~Match.~~	~~So, I'm right.~~
~~FO.~~	~~You're right.~~
Michael.	~~Wait.~~ You're the playwright?
Piddles.	The playwright?
FO.	And our roles, our job as characters is just as important in a play about our beloved cow as it is about any other adventure story ever told.

Michael.	You made all this. You wrote us.
Grim.	I'm just a writer.
Piddles.	And not just the keeper of death, but of life on this stage.
Grim.	I type what you become. I record your journey as it happens.
Match.	We know our tasks, but even for the best of us, it can get overwhelming and frustrating.
Grim.	~~But the same is true of humanity. We know our task, but even for the best of us, it can get overwhelming and frustrating.~~ But that's why we need you. By exploring what you do and who you become, we get to examine ourselves and our motives.
Man.	Is that why we're here?
Grim.	You are that which reflects the best of us.
Law.	Is that really true?
Grim.	Yes. You are that which reflects the best of us.
Michael.	(*to FO*) And you knew?
FO.	Well, I mentioned in the last play that I knew the playwright.
Montaño.	So, this is still real? We're still in the show?
Grim.	We are.
Montaño.	(looking out over the audience) But what if no one comes to watch the show?
Grim.	That's a possibility.
Piddles.	And what if people don't like it?
Grim.	That's a big possibility as well.
~~Law.~~	~~You mean some people may feel forced to watch it?~~
~~Grim.~~	~~That happens. Family. Contests.~~
~~Michael.~~	~~But our families are out there. Genetics or not. I can feel that this place is filled with family.~~
Grim.	~~More than you realize.~~ (*moves down left to watch the end of the show*) But there's something else ~~you need to realize.~~
~~Michael.~~	~~What's that?~~
FO.	This stage is filled with family.
Hatch.	The characters

101

Match.   Here for just a short moment in time

Agatha.   The actors portraying the characters

Man.   Becoming who they need to be in order to be faithful to the script

Law.   The light ~~technicians~~

SM.   And sound technicians

Piddles.   And the backstage crew

Michael.   ~~And yes,~~ all the people who support those on this stage

FO.   Working together, ~~even when they don't understand~~

Montaño.   Creating this beautiful, powerful thing called theatre

Piddles.   And we, as characters,

Agatha.   Play our parts

Hatch.   Whether it's in time-tested classics

Match.   Or in newer works

Michael.   Or in creating something totally fresh in both draft and final form

Piddles.   To understand

Man.   To appreciate

SM.   To celebrate

FO.   To proclaim that

ALL (*except Grim*)   This gift, this privilege to create

Piddles.   Is a duty and function

FO.   Of time

Hatch.   Time

Michael.   Time

Agatha.   And of art.

SM.   Art

Man.   Art

Michael.   Together in one moment, at one place, here

ALL (*except Grim*) On this stage.

Grim.   This stage.

ALL.   This stage.

Grim.   This moment.

ALL.   This moment.

Grim.   This fleeting moment

Michael.   That will never return.

Piddles.   Never.

Michael.   But will forever be.

Piddles.   Forever.

FO.   Forever.

Match.   Forever.

Grim.   And so, Stage Manager . . .

SM.   (*Stepping up*) Well, it's getting late here on this stage, at least for this play. We're
            to the end of the script for "The Beebles Refrain," a coming together again to
            figure out why we're here and what we're doing. But once again, I think we just
            might have figured it out. We hope you have, too. If you haven't, there's not
            much we can do about that, now is there? So, to all of you we say "good luck."

Everybody gasps.

Montaño.   You can't say that!

Montaño pulls out a baseball and throws it at SM, knocking him down and out.

~~Grim.   Montaño !~~

ALL.   Montaño.

Montaño.   I regret nothing.

The stage goes black.

Lowery Christopher Collins (Chris) has been an educator and writer for over thirty years. He is currently a professor of English at Panola College in Carthage, Texas. He has taught at the high school, middle school, and elementary school levels and as an English and literature instructor at the college and university level. For several years, he was a high school theatre director and a gifted education consultant. He's been honored with several teaching awards, including the Young Audiences of Northeast Texas Outstanding Service to the Profession Award and the Kennedy Center's Steven Sondheim Award for being one of the most "Inspirational Teachers" in the U.S.

He is also an award-winning playwright of over thirty scripts, a weekly newspaper columnist, a short story writer, a poet, a pianist, a vocalist, a songwriter, a recording artist with Daywind Studios, the founder and artistic director of Stagelands Theatre Company, an aspiring novelist, and a (former) choir director. He's taught a variety of classes, from rhetoric and composition to literature to acting to the Bible.

He holds a Bachelor of Arts Degree in English and History and a Master of Arts Degree in English from Stephen F. Austin State University in Texas and has served on fine arts and gifted education committees as well as on a board of governors for a small playhouse.

In addition to his interests in teaching, directing, and writing, he has a fondness for lighthouses, windmills, filmmaking, salsa, sculpture, Flannery O'Connor, travel, dominos, guacamole, social media, genetics, Maine, landscaping, pillows, gospel music, Shakespeare, marbles, YouTube, quantum physics, movies, weird jokes, maps, trees, cold rooms, and Texas.

He can be reached at mrchriscollins@hotmail.com,

on Facebook at www.facebook.com/tofferdreams,

on Twitter at "tofferdreams,"

and at his website:www.ChristopherCollinsOnline.com.

To view Christopher Collins's books and other writing, visit Ponderlake Publishing, at www.ponderlake.com.

SET SUGGESTIONS

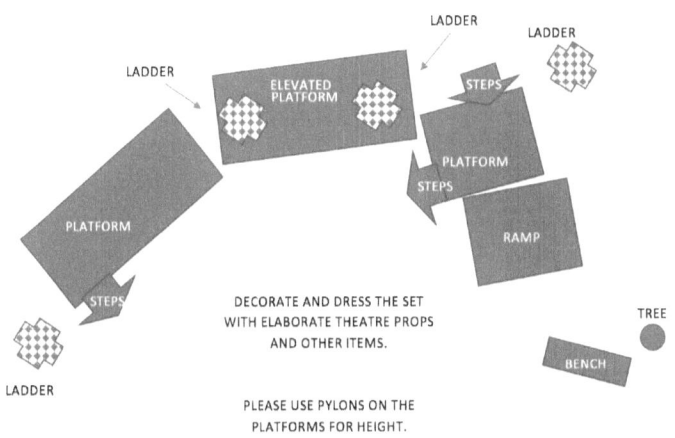

LADDER

LADDER

LADDER

ELEVATED PLATFORM

STEPS

PLATFORM

STEPS

PLATFORM

RAMP

STEPS

DECORATE AND DRESS THE SET
WITH ELABORATE THEATRE PROPS
AND OTHER ITEMS.

TREE

BENCH

LADDER

PLEASE USE PYLONS ON THE
PLATFORMS FOR HEIGHT.